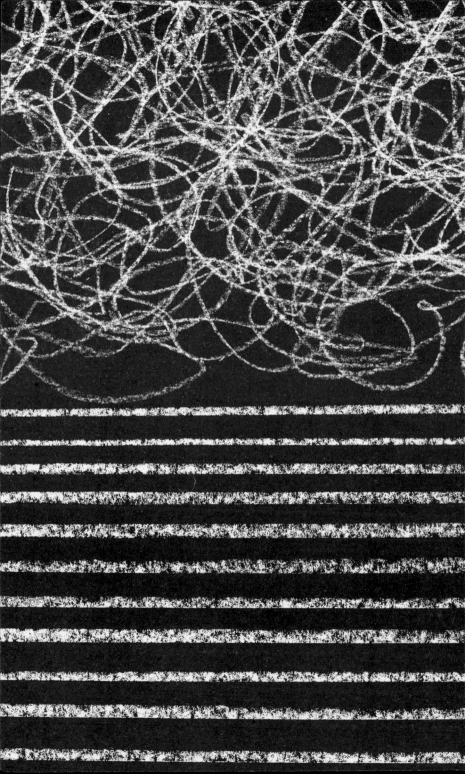

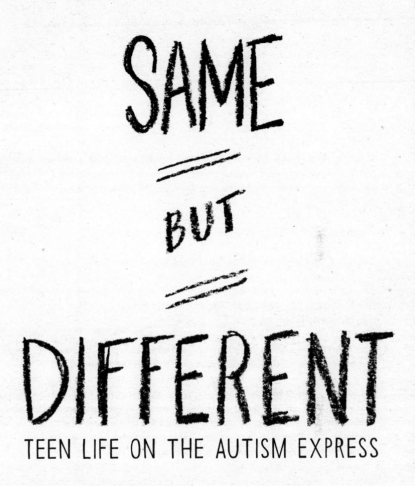

SAME

BUT

DIFFERENT

TEEN LIFE ON THE AUTISM EXPRESS

HOLLY ROBINSON PEETE
RYAN ELIZABETH PEETE · RJ PEETE

SCHOLASTIC INC.

This book was originally published in hardcover by Scholastic Press in 2016.

All rights reserved. Published by Scholastic Inc., *Publishers since 1920*. SCHOLASTIC and associated logos are trademarks and/or registered trademarks of Scholastic Inc.

The publisher does not have any control over and does not assume any responsibility for author or third-party websites or their content.

This book is a work of fiction. Names, characters, places, and incidents are either the product of the author's imagination or are used fictitiously, and any resemblance to actual persons, living or dead, business establishments, events, or locales is entirely coincidental.

ISBN 978-0-545-09469-6

10 9 8 7 6 5 4 3 2 1   18 19 20 21 22

Printed in the U.S.A.   40

First printing 2018

Book design by Mary Claire Cruz

*To those families who have allowed us
to weave their stories into ours, and who
have been guideposts along the way*

CONTENTS

WELCOME TO OUR JOURNEY ON THE AUTISM EXPRESS

A LETTER FROM MOM

Dear Ryan and RJ,

When your dad and I found out I was having twins, I knew we'd been given a double blessing. A girl and a boy. Two beautiful jewels born on the same day. RJ, you arrived two minutes before Ryan.

In January of 2000, when you were three years old, our world changed forever, when your pediatrician told Dad and me, "Your son has classic autism." We were crushed. We called that the Never Day because the doctor immediately listed all the "nevers" we could expect. She said you would never:

1. Have meaningful friendships
2. Play organized sports
3. Attend mainstream schools
4. Live on your own
5. Speak like a "normal" child

The list went on from there. The hardest blow, though, was when she told us that you, RJ, would never tell us that you loved us.

The irony about the diagnosis day—or D day, as we also called it—was that you, Ryan, insisted on being in the medical evaluation with RJ. Out of some twins' act of solidarity, you mimicked your brother during the evaluation, refusing eye contact with the doctor and playing alone instead of trying to engage RJ like you normally did. The doctor mistakenly determined you were both on the autism spectrum.

Imagine that. Even back then, you didn't want RJ to be alone with his autism.

RJ, I thought the autism label meant you wouldn't be able to go to school with Ryan, make friends, or enjoy sports with Dad.

The doctor tried to limit and define you with her diagnosis, but your sincere soul and inviting eyes refused to let her limitations stop you. As a young child, you flourished, took on challenges, and had many triumphs.

There were some scary times, though. Shortly

after your diagnosis, you "eloped"—an autism term we would become all too familiar with. You wandered off from our home and we couldn't find you for hours. We experienced a level of panic I didn't know existed. We combed the whole neighborhood and eventually found you sitting on the roof of our house, oblivious, and clutching your Thomas the Tank Engine train, intently spinning its wheels.

You surely heard us screaming your name, but back then, you were so verbally limited that you were unable to process the fear and urgency in our voices. That was a horrific day that turned into the best day—because we found you. And held you. And have been guiding and loving you, each and every day since that moment.

Your early school years have flown by quickly. And now, you and Ryan are in high school. You're a handsome young man, and your sister is a beautiful young woman. You have developed verbally. You can ask for what you want. Today, when you hear an urgent tone in my voice, you have learned to know when I mean business. You still have limitations, but you've come a million miles.

Now my mission is to get you to self-advocate all the time, with friends, or with cruel kids who are trying to dupe you, or with someone who is mocking you. Or with teachers or coaches who lose their patience because they have very little experience with autism.

Like all mommies, I wish I could protect you forever. Build a giant fortress around your heart, and stand guard like a sentry. But, also like all moms, I can't shield you forever.

Now that you're a high school student, your future is unfolding before us. The necessary bridge between youth and adulthood is a very scary process. That bridge is high aboveground, and rickety at times. And while you know you want to cross over, what's on the other side seems foggy and unreachable. This is true of teenage life *without* autism. Add in autism, and suddenly, the risks and dangers seem insurmountable. They're all part of the topsy-turvy ride you've both endured on what we've come to lovingly call the Autism Express.

Ryan, you've been such a shining support for your brother. But that's taken its toll, I know. Even with your support, our family has faced many challenges. My sweet daughter, I've watched you struggle with frustration, anger, fear. And I've witnessed you working through so many troubling emotions. It hasn't been easy at times.

And so, to help other teens and families feel less alone, you've been brave enough to share your experiences, strength, and hope along this unpredictable journey. On these pages, you've invited readers to come along through the uncharted teen waters of school, friends, body changes, dating, and so much more. I applaud your bravery in expressing yourselves so well, and in sharing such deep and true feelings.

Telling your story in alternating voices between a twin sister and brother, you guys came up with the idea to keep the fictional names we chose for the autism sibling picture book *My Brother Charlie*, which we three collaborated on when you were young children. Like *Same but Different*, that book is based on your experiences and those of other families we've met on the Autism Express. So, once again, we introduce readers to Callie—to represent a version of you, Ryan.

And for you, RJ, Charlie. In this book, your younger brothers, Roman and Robinson, are also in the mix. For the sake of this story, we've named them Chris and Cole.

The title of this book revealed itself through the revealing of who you are—same but different. As twins, you're similar in so many ways, and as teenagers, you share the same hopes, worries, anxieties, and dreams as kids all over the world. But you're also such beautiful budding individuals who are different in many ways.

Through your first-person vignettes, you present the good, the bad—and all that's in between—throughout these trying years. It's a challenge for families of children who have autism, for siblings of teens with autism, and for friends of teens with autism to find stories that resonate and ring true because they come from real-life, heart-and-soul experiences.

They say if you've met one kid with autism, you've met *one kid with autism*. Everyone is different. Autism isn't a cookie-cutter disorder. That's why we've collaborated on *Same but Different*.

Though inspired heavily and intimately by our personal family journey, *Same but Different* is a tapestry of collective experiences woven from our lives, as well as from those families we have been blessed to encounter along the way. One of the biggest gifts autism has given us has been the families we've met, cried with, rejoiced with, and grown stronger with as a result of our collective experiences. They have been an indispensable source of inspiration.

RJ, as you so often say, "I may have autism, but autism doesn't *have* me." I'm so proud of you and Ryan for holding hands along this path.

Ryan, thank you for being such an incredible sister and friend to your twin brother. Robinson and Roman, you two have been awesome brothers, who continue to demonstrate that you always have RJ's back. And thank you both for being courageous enough to peel back the curtain of your lives so that others can witness your journeys on the Autism Express.

I love you.

Mom

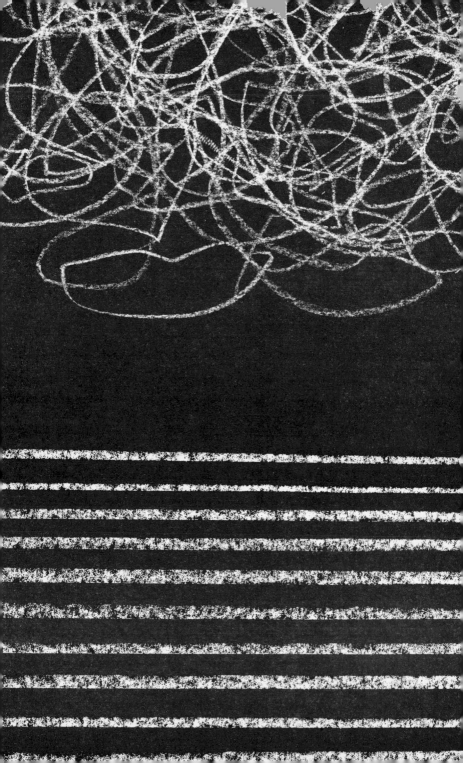

SPECIAL

CALLIE

I'M STARTING TENTH GRADE TODAY. The first day of school usually makes me feel excited, but this time around, things feel a little different. Simply because, well, things *are* different. My twin brother, Charlie, is starting ninth grade (again). Charlie's repeating a grade is a big deal. But it's much more than that. Charlie has autism. We've been together forever, and our tight bond is slowly loosening up. Charlie and I used to be inseparable. I knew he was different, but my younger brothers, Cole and Chris, and I have never

1

treated him that way. He's always been one of us, a member of the Garrison family. Nothing to it.

But then, I kept getting good grades, made lots of friends, joined the track team. Charlie didn't do any of those things. He had trouble finishing his homework, passing his classes, and answering questions in class. He wasn't the best at making friends, and let me tell you, my brother couldn't care less about playing on a sports team.

Charlie's repeating ninth grade. At the same time, he's watching me move ahead while he stays back. And okay, I admit it. I'm a little more than excited and relieved about not being in the same grade as Charlie. No more cringing when my "has-trouble-talking" brother is forced to speak out loud in class. No more volunteering to be his partner for class projects because no one else wants to. No more being known as "Charlie's sister." I can finally be me.

The thing is, though, Charlie and I are still in the same school building, so I can still see the stuff my brother goes through. Last year, I had a front-row seat to the action. Now I will witness it all from a distance. I can't help but wonder: Is it better to be up close, or to watch Charlie from farther back?

CHARLIE

OKAY. Here we go. First day is always the worst. New people. New routine. But this year, things suck even more. New people. Same place. Same grade, all over again. No Callie.

I'm cool with the no Callie part. That girl is always trying to jump into my business. Always telling me that she's my eyes and ears for when I need help "figuring it out." Well, guess what. I can "figure it out" without *her*.

Getting held back is even worse when you're made

3

to stay in special ed. Why do they call it special, anyway? There's nothing *special* about being in a place people say is "the loser room."

I'm sick of being *special*. I don't want to be *special* anymore.

I want to be in the main room in school. I mean, all I ever hear my parents talking about is getting me into the "mainstream." Well, there's nothing "main" about having kids look at you like you just farted. Is that why I'm special?

The good news is that I have Ms. Jackson this year for homeroom. The bad news is that Ms. Jackson was Callie's homeroom teacher last year. Turns out, Ms. Jackson also teaches special ed. That's good news, too. But as soon as I get into class, I hear people comparing me to the "normal twin." That's bad news. Callie's nowhere around? She's someplace in this big crowded school. She's off swimming in a mainstream. She's off being normal. Good for her. Miss Figure-It-Out is *figuring out* her own self, while I'm stuck here. Being special.

When the bell rings (that LOUD bell kills my

head), it's time to move to the next class. I somehow have to get to math. I hate changing rooms. I call it the torture race:

Go to my locker.

Struggle with the code.

Put back one set of books. Pull out another.

Kids all talking LOUDLY.

Strong smells.

Bad smells.

Bright lights that slice at me.

Colors that punch me in the eyes.

I wish I could wear my headphones at school, but it's against the rules. I'm a sweaty mess by the time I switch rooms. I didn't make it to the bathroom in between classes. So when I get to my next class, I need to pee. Badly.

But okay, things are back to being better when Justin and Steve sit by me. Callie had warned me that it might be hard to make friends this year, but I'm already doing it. With Steve and Justin. Right here. On each side. They're passing notes about the best-looking girls in our grade. And they're asking me to help move the notes around. And before I know it, I'm getting in trouble and being asked to sit up by the teacher. Justin and Steve don't admit to anything, but I don't care. I'm not sure how they didn't get caught. I guess I have to work on not being so loud when I fold paper. But who cares about that? I'm in with Steve and Justin. At least I have two friends. On the first day. What class was this again? Oh yeah, math.

Steve and Justin find me again during lunch and ask if I want to have pizza with them this Friday in the cafeteria, when there's going to be a back-to-school pizza menu. They ask if I have any money I can give them now to hold on to for Friday's pizza. I don't have any cash to give them today for the pizza, but they say I can bring it on Friday. Yes! Wait till I tell all of this to Callie.

The lunch bell rings, and we three walk to our next classes together. It's going to be a great year.

CALLIE

IT'S BEEN HAPPENING SINCE WE WERE LITTLE KIDS.
People who Charlie thinks are his "friends" and are
anything but. Here we are at the beginning of the
school year, and Charlie's so-called friends are starting in already.

Today I overhear those "friends" at lunch asking
Charlie to meet them on Friday for pizza, and to bring
fifty dollars. Now, math isn't my best subject, but I
will tell you that no pizza costs fifty dollars, not even
the kind with four cheeses.

7

So there I am in the cafeteria watching all of this, and wondering if I should step in or hang back. I'm always the one saving Charlie from stupid kids who are trying to mess with him. I'm so sick of doing it. And also, Charlie's sick of me doing it. He doesn't want a girl—me, his sister—sticking up for him. He thinks he can handle his "friends." The truth is, he mostly can't. But how can I stand there and let him be made to look like an idiot—again?

I want to jump in and tell Charlie that Steve and Justin are tricking him. I want to hear Charlie say, "Yeah, right," and joke with them like everyone knows what's really going on. But instead, I watch Charlie nod and say, "No problem. Fifty dollars. On Friday."

Ugh! He just doesn't get it. He can't see when people are taking advantage of him. Today I let it slide. But it's hard, because for so long, Charlie and I were what Mom calls peas in a pod. We did everything together. Now we're a grade apart, but it feels like so much more. And I don't think it's going to get any better soon.

I push Steve and Justin away from my mind and get out of the cafeteria as quickly and as quietly as I can, without Charlie knowing that his sis is in the picture.

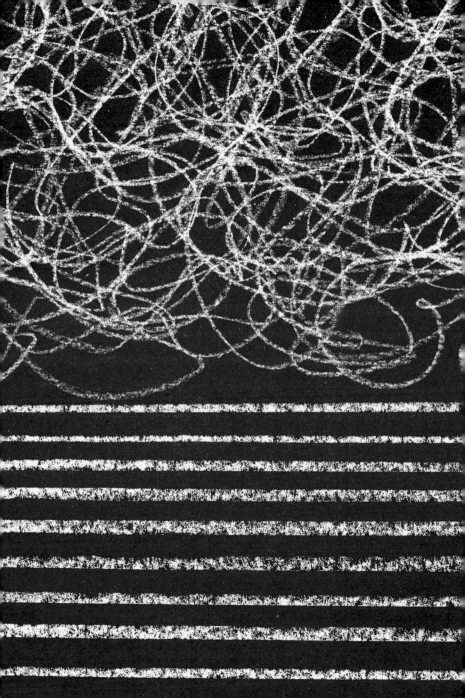

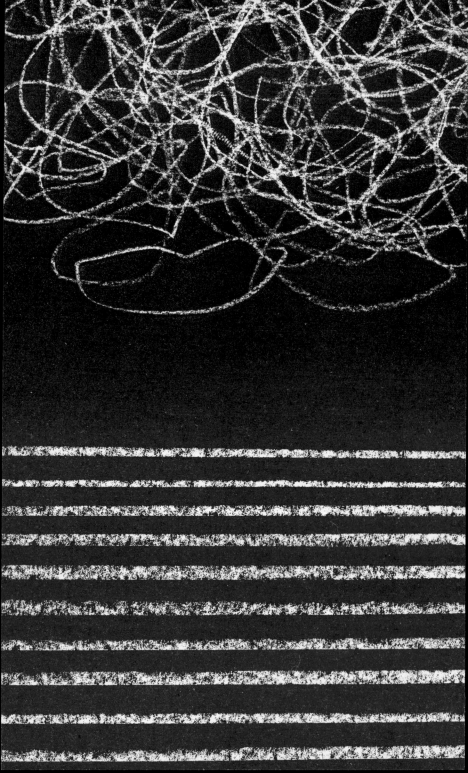

HAND CHECK

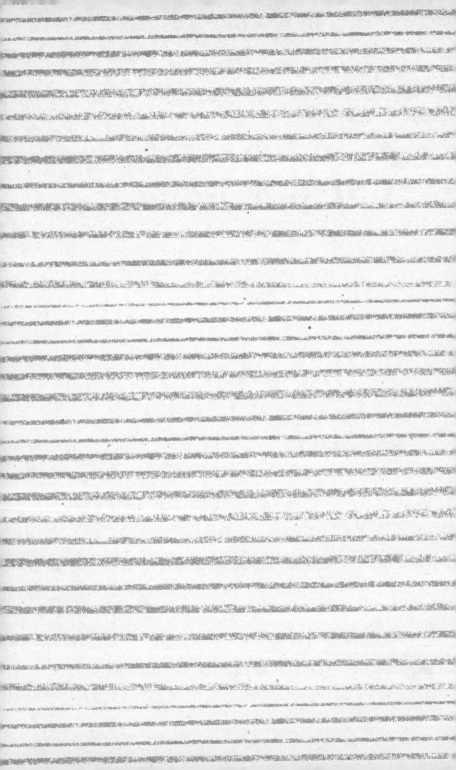

CALLIE

WHAT'S GOING ON? We're at the mall, for crying out loud, and Charlie's hands are in his pants. He needs new clothes for school—in a bad way. During the summer, he shot up to six feet tall. Usually, we'd never go to the mall on a school day. But since Charlie spent the whole summer in his hoodie and mesh soccer shorts, we had no idea his normal clothes made him look—well, let's just say if he continued to wear the mess he's got on today, those so-called friends of his wouldn't want to be seen with him.

This is the only reason I agree to go to the mall with Mom and Charlie, so he doesn't look like a homey in sweats. Plus, as Mom puts it, I'm beginning to "fill out." Which is a lame way of saying that, at age fifteen, I'm finally getting what look like boobs. This means I get new shirts. And real bras, which is awesome.

But for Charlie, body changes don't seem so awesome. I can tell by the way he's squirming and tugging at himself. He has no control over his own body. Today he's moodier than normal. His stupid hoodies are always hanging all over him, whether it's fifty degrees or a hundred. And my brother is always sweating because he yanks the hood on, and won't take it off, which means he looks weird on hot days like today. And did I mention that his sweat gives him total BO all day long?

This morning, I shoved some deodorant into his hands as we were scrambling to get ready for Day 1 at school. But the Extra Strength All-Day Wet Guard didn't go anyplace near his armpits, because Charlie threw the plastic bottle at me on his way out of the house. It skidded across the floor, leaving a white line of Extra Strength All-Day Wet Guard on the blue tiles. Well, at least our bathroom floor doesn't have BO. But still, this is why it's so hard to be Charlie's sister. Am I supposed to let him walk around smelling after he literally throws help in my face?

And then there's this hands-in-pants business. I shoot Charlie a killer look, wrench his arms by the elbows, and steer him toward the men's bathroom. He goes in to do whatever guys do in there. Of course, there's no line to get in (there's never a line for the men's room at the mall), so Charlie's gone right away.

Mom hovers by the men's room entrance. She closes her eyes and sighs. She tries to reason with me. "Honey, Charlie doesn't know what he doesn't know about himself. He *can't* know."

Yeah, yeah, *I* know that *Charlie* can't know. I've known this my whole life. But what I also *know* is that I'm tired of *him* not knowing that wherever we go, people look at us like we're some kind of weirdos.

Now I'm the one trying to reason with Mom. Can't she see the people in the mall are staring at this circus scene we're making? I say, "Well, Charlie *needs* to know, and *you* need to talk to him about it. What if my friends were here? What if they saw this whole thing?"

Mom looks like she's paying attention, but is she *hearing* me?

CHARLIE

I COME OUT OF THE BATHROOM, WONDERING WHAT IN THE WORLD I DID WRONG THIS TIME. Like this morning. Why would I smear anything on my body that smells like baby powder mixed with metal? Doesn't Callie understand that Wet Guard smells horrible? Maybe it's the All-Day part that gives it that funky smell.

And why do I need it, anyway? There's nothing wrong with my nose, and to me, I smell fine.

It's what's inside me that's making me feel like I need some all-day extra strength. My whole inside feels like a field full of fireworks that I can't stop from going off. It's scary. When the noise and sparks get really loud behind my eyes and in my belly and in my bones and veins, that's when I put on my hoodie, pull the hood closer, and wear my headphones. Even when they're unplugged, they feel good on my ears.

I overhear Mom telling Callie that the two of them will come back to the mall another day.

"Without Charlie," Mom says.

"Without hands-in-his-pants smelly-boy," Callie says.

I yank at the strings in my hoodie's hood. Tug hard. I whisper into the hood's warmth, "See if I care, All-Day Naggy Callie."

CALLIE

I GET TO GO TO THE MALL AGAIN TODAY AFTER SCHOOL. Thank the lord. No Charlie. No circus act. No smell. Mom and I are together, while Dad stays home with Charlie. Mom tells me they're gonna talk about "being a man."

I have my doubts this man-talk will go well. Dad is great with a football but not so great with his words sometimes. He's smart, and he loves all of us. But I've seen him get frustrated when he's talking to Charlie.

But whatever. All I care about at this moment is me and Mom. At the mall. Just us. Together.

The afternoon starts off great. We walk quickly through the mall and don't have to worry about leaving *him* behind. We take in the window displays without having to stop at each one. We walk a different route instead of the same way to the same stores in the same direction. We stop to have a snack when we're hungry, not when Charlie decides it's okay. We weave in and out of the people walking through the mall, not worried that Charlie will get nervous or scared.

It's okay if I take as long as I want to try on clothes. I don't have to cut anything short this afternoon. It's okay that Mom comes into the dressing room with me instead of standing guard near Charlie.

We're good just going with the flow. With Charlie there is no flow. Ever.

And then, as I'm trying on a really cute pair of jeans, and feeling free of my brother, he—well, the mention of him—finds his way back into what was supposed to be *my* afternoon, when Mom starts talking about what we can do to help him.

Oh God, Mom, no! I'm thinking. *He's not here. He's NOT here. We are away from him. Far away. You and me. And NOT him. Can we just have one day without Charlie?!*

But Mom starts in. She's talking about all the changes Charlie and I are going through. She says that it's even tougher for him because he's "a little out of whack" and can't "reel himself in."

To tell you the truth, Mom seems a little out of whack herself when she talks to me about this. So she starts in with how important it is to be part of "Team Charlie" and all the things *we're* going to do to help.

Mom goes through a kind of list:

"We" decide that Charlie needs more OT—occupational therapy.

And "we" agree that I'll go with him to the sessions two days a week to keep him company.

"We" determine that the one time we switched soaps, and Charlie hated it, was a mistake, and that "we" need to be careful when picking out things like soap and deodorant that Charlie might not like.

Because, as "we" know, kids with autism are often super sensitive to smells.

And so, our mother-daughter afternoon at the mall ends with a stop at the drugstore, where we buy out the entire shelf of different deodorants so Charlie can pick one out for himself at home.

When we walk into the house, I see Dad's profile— TV on, head in hands.

Mom says, "Did we have the talk?" As if all of us were talking about becoming a man.

Dad nods.

Maybe my father's the one who needs help to stop sweating now, and could use a bag of deodorant.

I run to my bedroom, away from this "we" scene.

CHARLIE

**DON'T ASK ME TO TELL YOU WHAT PEOPLE ARE FEEL-
ING FROM THE EXPRESSIONS ON THEIR FACES,
BECAUSE MOST OF THE TIME, I DON'T KNOW.**

But today I *can* tell that something weird is coming from Dad.

I can tell because he's walking back and forth.

And up and down the steps.

And hunching his shoulders a lot.

I try to avoid it by staying in my room, playing

video games, but it isn't long before I hear Dad's heavy feet come up the stairs.

Dad starts to talk about what men can and can't do. He talks about urges, about girls—I mean, he just goes on and on. And then when he notices that I sorta stop listening, he says, like he's mad at me, "And for God's sake, keep your hands out of your pants." Dad walks out of my room, like a storm has just started. He's moving fast, as if he's trying to run away from the rain.

Why is everybody so mad about me and my hands in my pants? I'm not doing anything with my hands. It's just like they belong there somehow. It's like putting them in a pocket that's next to my tummy.

I get back to my video game. Back to where things make sense. Back to where there are levels and points to get ahead. In a video game, I can win at least. Other places, I'm always the loser, it seems.

I hear a knock on the door, and I know it's Callie. She's doing our secret twins-knock. Three short knocks. Stop. Then three more short ones. Stop.

Callie walks in with a huge bag from Target that's dangling from her arm. *She* looks mad, too.

"What?" I say.

"*What?*" she copies me, and tosses the bag onto my bed.

CALLIE

"WHAT DID YOU DO TO DAD? He looks like he's swallowed a bug."

Charlie's ignoring me.

I take a deep breath, and go into "we" mode.

I tell him that maybe we should make some lists of what we should do during our morning routine, just to be sure we both remember to do everything we're supposed to do. And I suggest that we write down what we can and cannot do in public (as if *we* are both the ones with our hands in our pants).

I hate making these lists. They seem like they're for little kids. But Charlie doesn't seem to mind so much when I do the writing. It's better than Mom or Dad doing it, he says. So we start.

1. On school days, we agree to each take a shower, wash our hair for two minutes, our faces for a whole minute, and our bodies for a total of three minutes.

2. After drying off, we'll each brush our teeth (two minutes), hair (fifteen seconds), and put on the deodorant of his choice (fifteen seconds). There are some important things to add about hair. I get more time with my hair because I'm me, and girls need more hair time. We also agree that if Charlie's brushing his hair, and the brush starts to "claw" his scalp, he can stop. Ever since he was a little kid, Charlie's hated the brush. He calls it the lion claws. When we were really small, and Charlie couldn't talk as good, it was the worst. As soon as the brush came near his hair, the screaming would start. Now he can

at least tell us to stop. And, oh, does he tell us when those claws are doing too much digging!

3. On the weekends, we don't have to go through this whole minute-by-minute process right when we wake up, but it's gotta be done at some point during the day, and always before we leave the house.

Charlie's ready to quit the list after only the third thing. I know we should add something to the list about not having hands in pants, but I don't press it.

Still, Charlie starts sputtering about how the list is done, and we have to stick to THIS LIST, and there's no adding or subtracting from THIS LIST.

And THIS LIST is our final list.

And don't ever change THIS LIST.

And do I know that THIS LIST is it?

Charlie's hands are in his pants the whole time when he tells me all about THIS can't-ever-be-changed list.

I tell him this list is perfect.

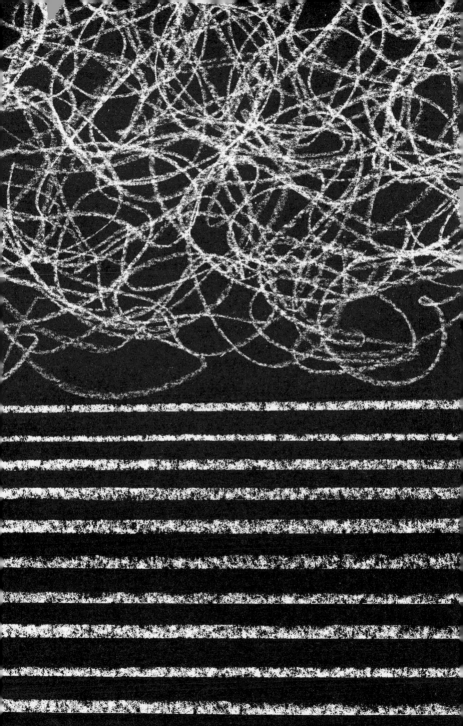

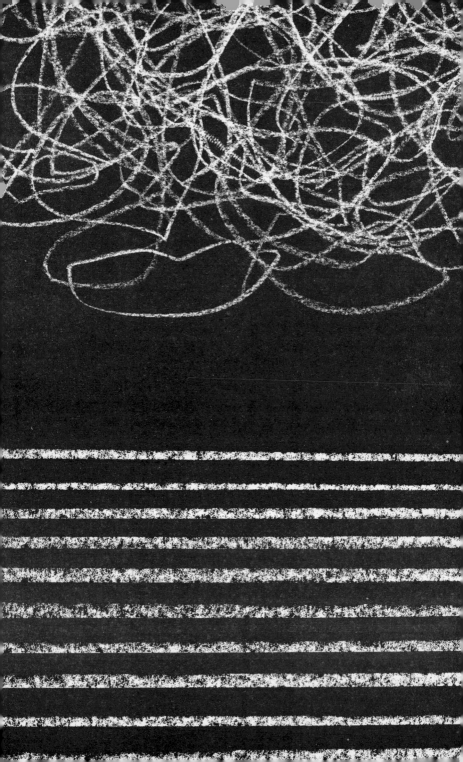

HEY, YOU,
WHY ME?

CALLIE

HEY, YOU, CHARLIE! I would never in a million years ask this to your face.

But I ask it to my own face a lot when I look into the mirror: *Why me?*

Why did I have to be born the twin of a brother like you?

Why do I have to be the strong one?

Why am I the one who flies in on a rescue helicopter again and again and again to save you from whatever bug or hairbrush or insult is flying in your direction?

Why me?

Why do I have to be so tough?

Why am I always expected to be the "good" twin?

Why can't I have it my way all the time, like you get? All the time.

Why do I turn up my music and get yelled at by Dad? But when you play your music way too loud, no one blinks or asks anything of you. It's as if that music belongs to you, when the music I like to blast, because I enjoy singing to it, is shut down before it can be mine.

Hey, you. Why me?

Why, since we were little kids, have I had to put up with you ruining my playdates?

Hey, you, Charlie. Remember that? Those playdates when you got fixated on a certain toy and would hug that Lego or stuffed dog or plastic fire truck like it was a part of your body. And nobody else could come near it. And no other kid would dare try to take it away, for fear that you'd go off on one of your screeching meltdowns.

Why did we turn into the twins who could only have playdates at home?

Why was I always forced to have playdates that included you?

Why was going to another kid's birthday party at his house always such a hassle?

Why am I the daughter of a mom who smiles too much when other parents are in the room with you and me?

Why, after all these years, when we don't even have playdates anymore, am I still angry about them?

Why hasn't much changed since those days?

Now when we have friends over, why am I the one made to drag you away from your dumb video games so that you can (as Mom who smiles too much says) "practice socializing"?

Hey, you. Why me?

Why do I know exactly what you like and what you hate, without having to ask?

Why am I the one who can pick out the best birthday gifts, and know you will love my presents more than anything?

Mom says this is the "beauty of being a twin." But there are times when this so-called beauty seems pretty ugly.

Charlie and I are almost too close, sometimes. When he's hurting, I'm hurting. And when he does something mean to me, it's the most painful thing ever. Lots of times Charlie doesn't even know when he's being hurtful, and that makes it even harder to bear. And it makes all the whys louder.

Why does Charlie embarrass me so much in front of strangers, like when he says things loudly that don't really make sense?

Why do I have the brother who walks up to talk to people when they're totally not interested?

Why am I the twin sister of the kid who wanders off away from us when we're not paying close attention?

Why do I have to deal with Charlie always wanting things the exact way he wants them when he wants them (and sounding like a whiny brat to people who don't know the whole story)?

Hey, you, Charlie. Why me?

If I did ever have the guts to ask you these things to your face, you'd probably just look and wonder why I'm asking. But I can't help it. The whys won't leave me alone. And sometimes they're really loud.

Why do I have to have the brother who's gotten held back at school?

Why am I the one who has to stay close to him to make sure he doesn't get into too much trouble or that people don't take advantage of him?

Why am I always watching out for someone who is the same age as me?

Why am I so tired of asking *Why me*?

Why, when I'm really hungry at dinnertime, do we all have to wait to eat until you come to the table because you're in a bad mood or don't like the smell of the food?

And why do you even have autism, anyway?

And hey, you, since there's so much "beauty of being twins" between us, why don't *I* have autism?

CHARLIE

WHY ME?

Is that even a real question?

On tests at school, they ask questions. But no test ever asks me to answer *Why me?*

I guess it's a real question, because I ask it a lot.

Why have I always had to hang out with Callie, even when I don't want to? (Okay, PS, maybe that's what twins do, but for how long? It's still going on, this always-having-to-be-together thing.)

Why have I had to always be included in her

friends' playdates at our house when I don't give a crap about those girls and their stupid giggles and combing dolls' hair? (PS, how lame is that?)

Why, on these playdates, did Mom always have to hang close by?

Why was Mom always frowning and looking scared during these playdates? (PS, what's scary about dolls with long hair?)

Why does Callie never want me to hang out with her and her friends? (PS, Doesn't she get it that I don't want to hang out with her friends anymore, anyway?)

Why did I have to get held back a grade? (PS, I'm not stupid. So why do they think I am?)

Why can't people see that I have my own friends?

Why won't they realize that I don't want to go to the mall together? That I seriously have my own life, and I think it's pretty sweet?

Why will they not understand that I don't need anyone to force me away from my video games and my favorite old-school hip-hop music?

Why don't they get me?

Is that a real question?

CALLIE

HEY, YOU, CHARLIE. I'm probably not the only one in our family asking why.

I bet our younger brothers, Chris and Cole, want to know the same things. But I'm so sick of asking *Why me?* that I don't want to drag them into my own personal world of guilt. I don't want to spread the weight I feel on my shoulders to my younger brothers. So I don't bring it up. Besides, they're in middle school. And boys. Boys in middle school don't ask stuff like that, I don't think.

And, yeah, that reminds me, why am I the only freakin' girl in our family?

And why does that suck so bad? Actually, this is a *why* I can answer. I have no one to hang out with at home—that's why it sucks!

Okay, there's Mom to hang out with, but that's not real hanging out. That's going to the mall with your mother, and not talking to her about what's really on your mind—boys, my boobs, when will I get my period, and what does kissing a boy feel like, and if you kiss a boy when you have your period, will you get a disease?

Mom is great at shopping and doing my hair, but seriously, I would rather be doing that kind of stuff with a sister who knows what's cool before I have to tell her.

But why, why, why am I instead living in a house that's full of football and boys, and a brother whose hand lives in his pants?

Why did I get all the luck?

Three brothers.

One of them is autistic.

No sisters.

Why?

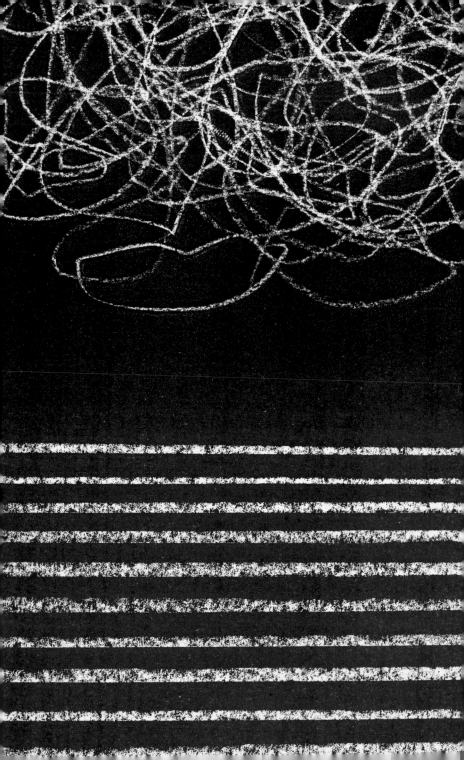

THE A-WORD

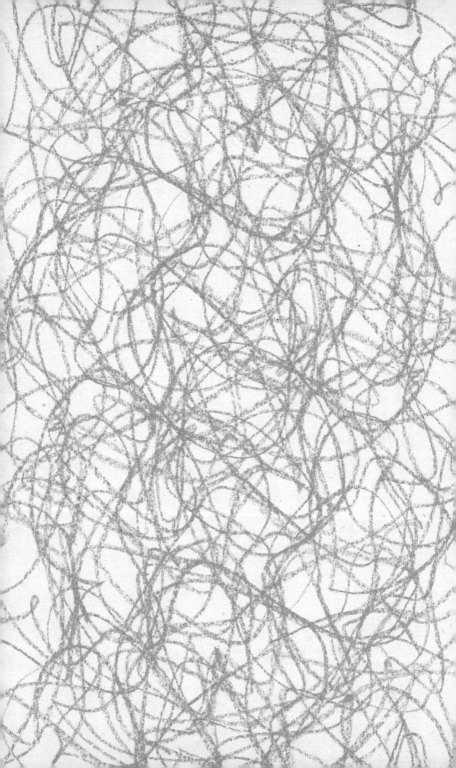

CHARLIE

WHY DO PEOPLE SAY I'M *AUTISTIC*?

I hate that word. So does Mom. She says *autistic* makes the hairs on the back of her neck stand up. (PS, who even has hair on their neck?)

I think Mom got her hatred of the A-word from me.

When I was eight years old, and finally starting to talk, one of the first things I said was, "I am not autism." Mom thought I was trying to say, "I am not autistic."

She was right. That's what I meant.

CALLIE

I GET THAT CHARLIE AND MOM DON'T LOVE THE WORD
AUTISTIC.

But a word is just a word, and what does it really matter?

Mom was a psych major in college. She loves to remind us that *autism* isn't "child-first language," whatever that means.

Mom says *autism* is like labeling and defining Charlie before you even get to know him. She says that calling Charlie autistic implies that Charlie *is* autism, rather than that he *has* autism.

Okay, psych major Mom, I get it. And Charlie's got it, too.

He's *got* autism.

Whatever *it* is.

CHARLIE

AS MUCH AS CALLIE GETS ON MY NERVES, I'LL ADMIT THAT SHE UNDERSTANDS ME THE BEST OF ANYONE. Chris and Cole don't get me as good as Callie does. She says it's a twin thing, but why does my sister know me better than my brothers? And why don't I understand her as much as she does me?

Like, she better not talk to me about girl stuff. I don't even know what *girl stuff* means, but she's on the phone a lot with her friends and tells me I can't listen because it's "girl stuff."

Why doesn't any guy in my family really know me like my sister, a girl with her "stuff," does?

Dad, Cole, and Chris, all they care about is wanting me to play football with them outside, or do what they want. But can't they just respect that I'm me? At least Callie does that. It's just lame that it's Callie and her girl stuff that's looking out for me.

CALLIE

SOMETIMES, I REALLY DON'T WANT TO EAT GLUTEN-FREE. I want to eat real pasta, and pizza crust. And cookies that taste normal.

But when your brother has autism, the whole family is on a strict gluten-free diet of quinoa and rice pasta, and some kind of cardboardy stuff they say is pizza crust. Somehow gluten sends Charlie into a spiral of acting out.

And so, Mom, whose smile is the same as when we were little kids on playdates with other parents around, continues to smile when she tries to convince us that bread and pizza crust made out of rice, and corn-flour spaghetti, tastes the same as the real food they're pretending to be.

What a lie.

The thing is, Charlie doesn't even know that the food world in our house stops spinning when he's around. He has no clue about the kind of special attention he gets from Mom and Dad, when it comes to eating.

Really when it comes to everything.

Like the way we all work around our schedules to get him to OT, to prep him for new things or places, to make sure he's comfortable, and safe, and not too stirred up, and won't come into contact with anything or anyone who might rock his autism boat.

My brother *with* autism *has* it all. And he doesn't even know it.

CHARLIE

CALLIE LOVES TO SAY IT'S ALL ABOUT ME.

Well, guess what, sister, it's not.

If it were all about me, I'd do whatever I want, whenever I want.

I would not want to go to school.

I would want to go to the zoo or aquarium all day long.

I would want to eat pizza with a real crust.

But, *noooo*, I *have* autism. So I never *get* what I want.

CALLIE

EVEN THOUGH THE SCHOOL YEAR HAS JUST STARTED, WE'RE ALREADY TALKING ABOUT OUR WINTER VACATION.

We always have to plan months in advance. I don't mind that. It gives me something to look forward to, when it's not going to be all about Charlie.

On vacation, we'll be more free to come and go as we please, without sticking to our airtight Charlie schedule.

But—we have to first *get* to the vacation, which

means we're already talking at home about the airport, the security check-ins, the flight, the hotel, and any kinds of challenges Charlie might have away from home.

Charlie's eyes look nervous when we even start this conversation. I bet my eyes get nervous, too, because I know I'm the one who is going to have to calm him down. I'm the one who will make sure Charlie knows what's going on, and is comfortable.

Sometimes I feel like Charlie's mother. But it's more than that. I'm his twin. We were both inside our mom, sharing her. It's always been that way, and still is.

CHARLIE

WHY DOES IT ALWAYS SEEM LIKE I HAVE TWO MOMS AT HOME?

I have Mom, and I have Callie, who's like a mom my same age.

Well, bump that.

I don't need two moms.

CALLIE

DOES CHARLIE REALLY *HAVE IT ALL*?

I mean, he *has* autism. And because of that, he has a lot of things I'm glad I don't have.

Would I want what he has, really?

No way.

What Charlie *has* is rough. And I would never admit it to him, but he's braver than I am, or will ever be.

Charlie has to live inside his own scrambled head and knotted body, with his own demons.

I can't imagine having *that*.

CHARLIE

EVEN THOUGH I HAVE AUTISM, AUTISM DOESN'T HAVE ME.

Mom loves when I say that, so I say that when she's around, and frowning, to make her happy.

But sometimes I feel like the A-word *does* have me.

Or stuff that comes with having autism—that stuff has got me tied up. Stuck.

There's the strange looks I get from people who don't know me.

There's the OT sessions I can't miss.

The special (disgusting) gluten-free diet.

Being held back in school.

And that's just some of the crap that's got me in the A-grip.

There's also the *not* being understood by kids and teachers, and my own brothers and dad, who just don't get me.

I'd change a lot of what comes with having autism.

But as much as I complain about my two moms, and Chris and Cole, and Dad, I wouldn't change my family. Because I do know they've got my back.

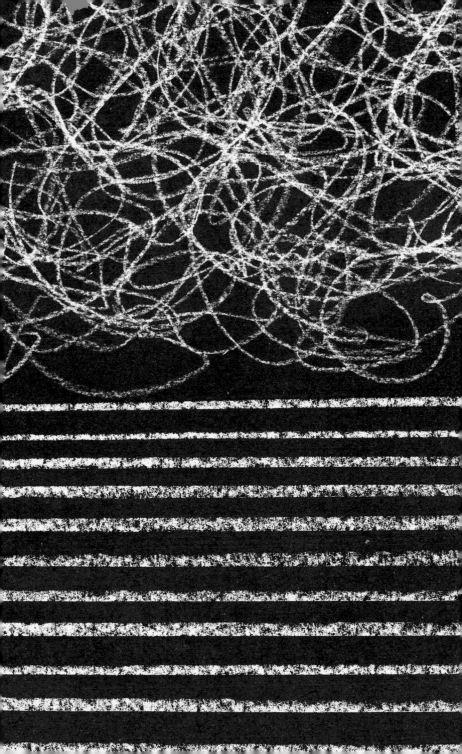

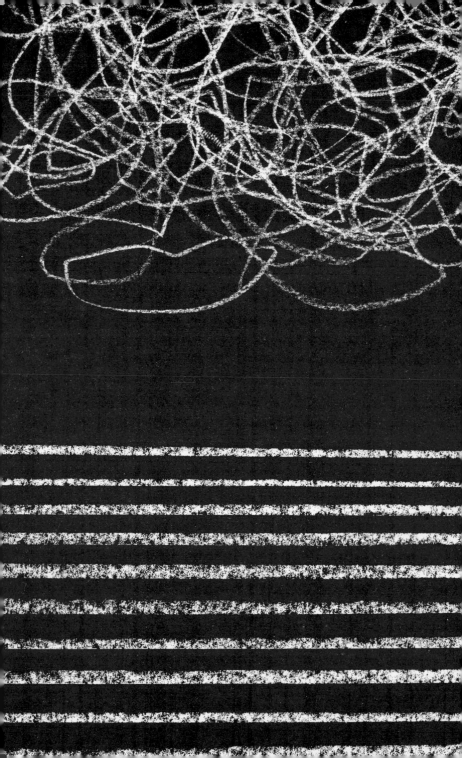

FIFTY BUCKS
FOR A PIZZA

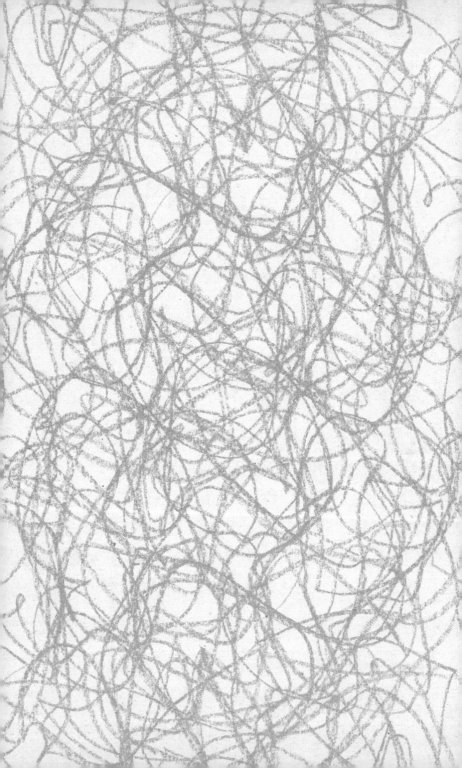

CHARLIE

I ASK MOM FOR LUNCH MONEY, AND SHE HANDS ME TEN DOLLARS FOR THE PIZZA. I tell her about Justin and Steve, and that I need fifty dollars. But Mom will only give me ten bucks.

How come she's so against me? She's just like Callie, not wanting me to make friends. I try to explain that Steve and Justin told me that the pizza costs more this year, but Mom doesn't believe me. She just doesn't want me to hang out with Steve and Justin. That's what it is.

Okay, so I ask Dad for pizza money, too, and he only gives me five dollars. But I don't care. I have a jar full of cash in my room from my allowance that I've been saving.

I show up the next day at school, and head over to what I already think of as "our spot" at lunch, ready to hand over the money to Justin and Steve, and out of nowhere, Callie shows up. She's practically invisible sometimes, then floats in like a butterfly.

Anyway, just as I'm telling her to back off and go hang out with *her* friends, Steve and Justin want to talk to my sister, probably because she's an older girl and they have to be nice to her because we're related.

But I say to Callie, "Bye. You can go now."

She's slow to walk away.

CALLIE

WELCOME TO WHAT I CALL *THE CHARLIE SHOW*.

Or maybe I should call it *Who Are Charlie's Real Friends?*

In this episode my brother gets duped. Well, in many episodes he gets scammed, and has no idea that it's happening.

I am fuming. So mad that I have to control myself so I don't yell and scream and stomp when I go back to the table to sit with my friends Lisa and Jillian.

But here's the thing. Charlie is never going to be totally independent of me. Not ever. Because if I don't protect him, if I can't stay close enough to see and hear what's going on, to shield him from the bad, then who will?

And how can my brother learn what's right and what's wrong if nobody points out that he's being played for a fool?

As always, today Charlie is the star of his show. That's because he's Charlie, and the world revolves around him, especially on days like today, when I stand by and watch his "friends" punk him.

It's the last day of the first week at school. Steve and Justin are back—and *The Charlie Show* begins.

You'd think Charlie would have enough sense to know that he can't even eat pizza at school because of its real-flour crust that makes him irritable and gives him a headache. But he's cleaned out the cash from his money jar at home (where he was saving to buy things on our winter vacation).

I'm sitting across the cafeteria by the windows with Lisa and Jillian, who are real friends of mine and would never, in a million years, ask me to bring fifty dollars to school to buy pizza. They're eating fries and drinking chocolate milk, while I watch *The Charlie Show.*

I see my brother take a wad of cash out of his knapsack, then dump a bunch of quarters, nickels, dimes, and pennies onto the lunch table, where Justin and Steve scoop them up faster than my own friends are slurping their chocolate milk.

They're stuffing the money into their own knapsacks and pockets before getting into the food line to buy the fifty-dollar pizza. Charlie follows them, but I notice they've somehow convinced him to stay at the table.

My neck starts to get hot. I want to go over there. I want to shake Charlie. I want to yell, "Don't you see what's going on?!" But I don't. I let this reality TV moment in my brother's life play out.

It's so hard to watch, though. I wish I could hit the remote, change the channel, and get onto something better.

Something that doesn't have bold credits rolling up the screen that say,

"Starring Callie's autistic brother, Charlie."

When Justin and Steve come back, they've got three slices of pizza. They high-five each other, and start to eat. Charlie puts his hand up for a high five. They at least give him that. Steve and Justin start to chow down on their pizza. Charlie is so busy trying to get them to high-five again that he's not eating. It's like he's forgotten about the pizza and the money. He just wants to high-five. I can see that his "friends" are way past that, ignoring Charlie and starting in on Charlie's slice while he's not getting the clue that the high five ended ten minutes ago. I look at the clock on the wall and notice that lunch period is going to be over in a few minutes, and Charlie will not have eaten, which means he'll be hungry and cranky and acting more stupid.

And then something cool happens. My friend Jillian has known me and Charlie since preschool. She's one of those girls who put up with many ruined playdates we had when we were little, and Charlie would come crashing down on one of our doll parties. She knows all about Charlie.

Jillian says, "Callie, isn't that your brother over there?"

I nod as if I'm noticing Charlie for the first time. "Oh yeah, that's him," I say, all nonchalant.

Jillian says, "Isn't he not supposed to be eating school pizza?"

"Yeah, right, whatever." I'm still trying to play it cool.

Jillian says, "I have some grapes and rice cakes that my mom made me bring to school today, and I don't want them, and my mother told me not to waste the food she packs me."

I nod again.

Jillian starts to walk over to Charlie's table with her grapes and rice cakes. I want to follow, but don't. I'm eager to play Sister-Mom in this episode of *The Charlie Show* or the *Who Are Charlie's Real Friends?* reality TV loop, but Jillian has taken the part away from me!

Next thing I know, she's giving Charlie her food, and he's eating it. And she gives my brother a high five. And a second high five, and a third when his hand comes back for more.

Then Jillian does something so awesome. She puts one hand out, palm up, in front of Steve and Justin and points to their knapsacks with her other hand.

They shrug. Jillian parks both her hands on her hips, and stares hard.

That's when my brother's "friends" start to hand over my brother's money to *my* friend, who brings it back to me at our girls' table, and gives me the highest high five ever.

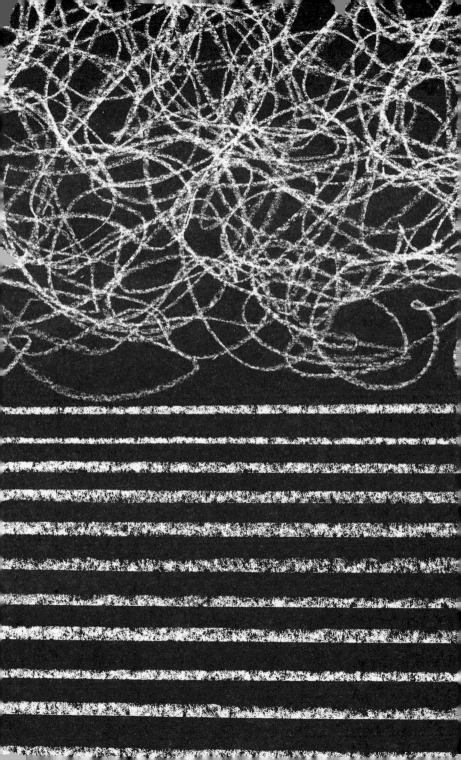

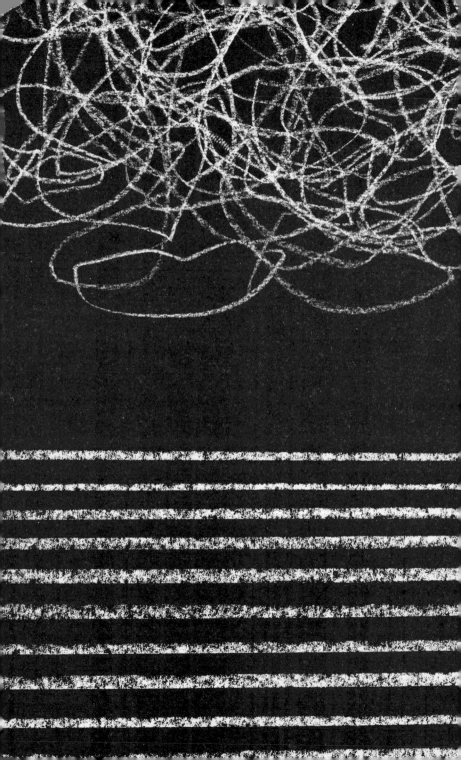

THE CHARLIE 411

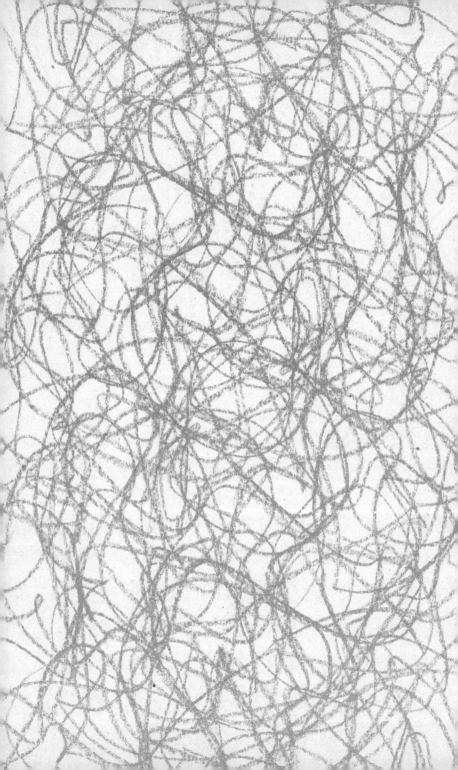

CHARLIE

**I'VE MADE IT THROUGH TWO WHOLE WEEKS AT
SCHOOL WHEN THE TROUBLE IN MY HOMEROOM
STARTS.**

At the end of homeroom, I have one foot out the
door, when Ms. Jackson calls my name. All I can
think is, *What was I doing wrong?*

I check myself. *Did I talk out loud? Or get up
without asking? Or fidget too much in my seat?* I
answer no, no, and no to all these questions.

But there's gotta be something. There's always something. And I always come up blank when I'm trying to figure out what I did *this* time. I never seem to know when something is my fault, or not.

I tell Ms. Jackson that I'm gonna be late for my next class. But she quickly tells me she'll write a note to my science teacher explaining why I'm late. I'm annoyed because we both know that science is one of my best classes. And walking in late with a note—everyone knows you are in trouble because of something.

Ms. Jackson wants to know how school has been for me in these early days. And she points out that a few times I've gotten up out of my seat without being called on.

"How can we work together on your behavior?" she wants to know.

What a dumb question. But at least she asks it. Most teachers think I'm being "disrespectful" or "uninterested"—as they've loved to say on my report cards.

The truth is, we can't work together unless Ms.

Jackson is willing to let me do school how I do best in school.

I want to tell her what I need, but somehow the words can't come out.

I want to let Ms. Jackson know I like—need—to get up out of my seat sometimes. That I don't like to be put on the spot. That sometimes—lots of times—I blurt things out that have nothing to do with what we're talking about in class. I don't mean to, but it just happens, and I can't help it.

I don't say any of this. Instead, I just tell Ms. Jackson, "My sister can probably tell you how we can work together. Ask Callie."

I snag the note out of Ms. Jackson's hand and race to science. I don't even notice what's going on in the class, just shove the note into Mr. Broderick's hands and fall into my seat. Justin and Steve give me a thumbs-up, for what, I'm not sure, and then Mr. Broderick says, "Shall we continue?" And he does.

CALLIE

I HATE TO CRY AT SCHOOL, BUT TODAY I DO.

I'm hanging out with my friends between periods, when I can't help but notice Ms. Jackson, Charlie's homeroom teacher. She's doing one of those moves when it appears you're not looking for someone but you are.

I catch her drift, and walk over. All I can think is, *What has Charlie done now?* It's not even a month since school started, and I'm actually surprised I haven't heard of him getting in trouble until today.

Ms. Jackson quietly asks if we can meet to talk about Charlie.

The sooner she knows about what she's getting into by having my brother as her student, the better.

I say, "Let's get it over with."

I'm used to this, so I want to just have the conversation, head-on.

Most people don't know a lot about autism, and I'm the one they come to when they want the 411 on how to deal with Charlie. They want the backstory so they can help Charlie—or help themselves help Charlie. Or at least put up with Charlie. Or figure out Charlie, which nobody can ever really do.

I've given the Charlie 411 backstory explanation so many times that I never get annoyed or frustrated when talking about autism. It's what I do. And I'm good at it.

Ms. Jackson and I start to walk to her classroom, and I begin to tell her what she needs to know about my brother.

How Charlie has always been different from my other brothers and me.

How autism makes Charlie act a little differently

from the other kids—well, a lot different from other kids, actually.

How Charlie is super smart about knowing what animals are feeling. And super smart when it comes to music and playing the piano. And super good at swimming. But that Charlie's not always school smart.

I explain that English and anything that has to do with language and words is hard for him. Math and science are easy for Charlie. It's actually scary how smart my brother is with math and science stuff. I mean, he's like a genius when it comes to memorizing facts about numbers, rocks, the human body, and planets.

Ms. Jackson is writing things down as I talk.

I tell her how Charlie doesn't understand when people are being sarcastic, or when something has a double meaning, or when a joke is one of those tongue-in-cheek kind, when you have to know about other things to get the joke.

Like, if someone says, "That test at school was a piece of cake," Charlie doesn't understand that means the test was easy. He thinks "piece of cake" is a silly comment about cake, and what does cake have to do with a test at school? Or if I say, "Don't cry over spilled milk," Charlie might wonder why we're talking about milk when he's drinking soda.

"So," I tell Ms. Jackson, "you should never say those kinds of things in class. Charlie will crack up at something that's not really a joke. Then everyone will crack up at Charlie because he's not connecting the dots."

When I explain to Ms. Jackson that Charlie trusts people too easily, and that he's not smart about reading people and situations, and that he's been the butt of joke after joke after joke—that's when I start to feel my throat get a stone in it, and pressure come from the back of my eyes, like something's pushing against my insides. That's when I start to cry. And it's not a little crying, either. The tears come on like a warm flood of something I can't totally explain. Because I've never once cried while giving anybody the Charlie 411.

I'm not totally sure *why* I'm crying, but I am, and I can't stop. And I can't look at Ms. Jackson, who's snapping tissues out of the tissue box she keeps on her desk for when kids sneeze. Her hand is rubbing slow circles on my back.

"Thank you, Callie," she says quietly. "Thank you for being brave and honest and generous."

I nod, but I still can't look at her.

"I hope what I'm telling you about Charlie helps you" is all I can manage to say.

Ms. Jackson says, "I hope it helps you, too, Callie."

Later, at home, I talk to Mom alone about my conversation with Ms. Jackson. When I tell her about my tears, I realize why I cried so much. "I miss being able to help Charlie at school. I'm worried that my talk with Ms. Jackson isn't enough."

Mom's listening carefully.

I say, "I like Ms. Jackson, but who's going to really protect Charlie?" Usually, I'm his extra eyes at school. People don't mess with him because they know my friends and I won't stand for it. Plus, most of us have been in the same class with Charlie forever. In the past, when a new kid came to school, I would always find a way to partner up on a project with that kid early in the semester so that I could share the Charlie 411 about autism.

I start to cry—again. At least I can look at Mom when I ask, "How am I going to find a way to be a part of Charlie's life at school without making him feel babied or stupid, and without being like sister-hawk, always flying overhead, looking out? And also, who's gonna explain to kids the real deal on Charlie?"

Mom's thinking now. I can see it in the way she's biting at her bottom lip.

She comes up with a great idea, which is to have someone else come into the classroom to talk about differences, and teamwork and compassion and bully-ing, and all the things that can help Charlie but not make him feel dumb and like the whole world is baby-ing him.

Mom says, "If another person, other than you, Callie, gives the 411, then sister-hawk would be off the hook."

I look at Mom with a tearstained face. "Sister-hawk would love a vacation," I say, and we both laugh.

The next day after school, I tell Ms. Jackson Mom's idea. She thinks it's a good one, and by the next week, she's got someone lined up.

I explain to Ms. Jackson about sister-hawk needing to give her eagle eye and her wings a rest, and how I want to be totally left out of the planning details of the speaker so that if Charlie asks, I can honestly say I have no idea what he's talking about.

CHARLIE

SOMETHING'S GOING ON. It's the third week of school, and we're having what Ms. Jackson is calling a motivational speaker come to our class. She says it's someone to help us "work together, and to recognize and celebrate our differences."

The last time this happened was when I was in sixth grade, and this motivational-speaker lady came to our school to talk about "getting along" and it turned into really coming to talk about being in a class with a person who has autism. And when she was speaking, everyone kept looking over at me.

I'm not stupid, and I wish people would stop treating me like that. I know this has to do with me. But I don't say anything, because Ms. Jackson seems really excited about it. It's weird. Most of the kids are smiling when Ms. Jackson tells us that the speaker is coming. Probably because we're missing math. Why can't we ever be missing English?

The speaker starts off by telling how he was painfully shy growing up and didn't talk in class and hated to read out loud. Words in books didn't make sense to him. Turns out, he's dyslexic, which makes it super hard for him to read. He hated going to school. Sat in the back.

This guy has dumb pants on that are wrinkled, and ugly shoes, and teeth like they're stained with coffee. But when he begins to talk about getting in trouble a lot at school for looking like he wasn't paying attention in class, I start to listen. And when he tells us how being smart at science made him want to learn, I'm thinking this guy is okay. He says he started to get really good at science when he got a tutor, and now he's a surgeon.

"That's my story," he says to the class. "What's yours?"

This dyslexic doctor wants to know what's hard for us, what would make things easier in our lives, and how we're dealing with our struggles.

Of course nobody raises their hand. Inside, I'm like, *Dude, we're in ninth grade and we just met you, and it's the first few weeks of school, and nobody's gonna say anything about struggles, not even the girls.*

Ms. Jackson instead asks each of us to write out a truth—a challenge or a problem we have—on a piece of paper that she'll then read out loud so we can "work together to find a solution." She promises not to tell who's written each paper. "This will be an anonymous exercise," she says.

The kids in my class surprise me with what they've written, even though I don't know who's written what. Some people have written about weight problems. Others about hard times with their parents. One kid admits that's he's really bad at math, and always feels stupid. I'm so into what Ms. Jackson is reading from this kid's paper (because being *good* at math is what makes me feel *not* stupid), that I'm caught off guard. Ms. Jackson gets to mine. "My truth," she reads, "is that I wish I could know when people were teasing me or not."

I look around to see who's doing what as my teacher is telling everyone about what's hard for me. Nobody's looking in my direction or even giggling. Kids are just listening. One kid, he's nodding like Ms. Jackson is reading from *his* paper.

But still, after class is over, for the rest of the day, I can't shake the feeling that everyone will know that was *my* paper.

That night in bed, I'm still thinking about what happened in school, and how Callie tells me I trust people too easily, and that I don't stick up for myself.

But today in Ms. Jackson's class, I trusted that speaker. And I didn't even have to stick up for myself when Ms. Jackson read from my paper.

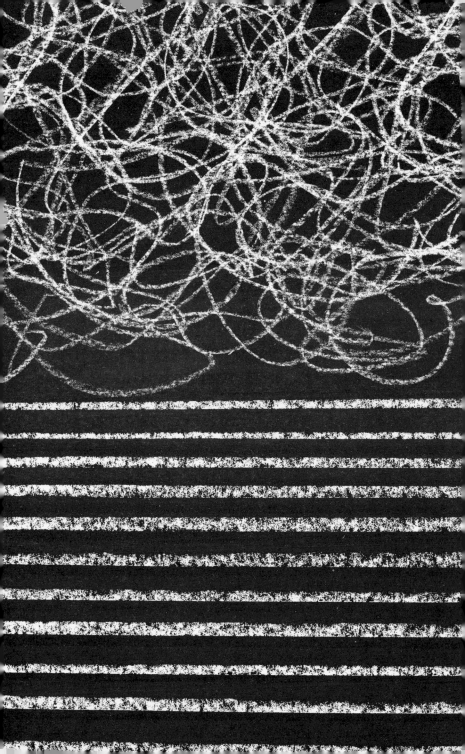

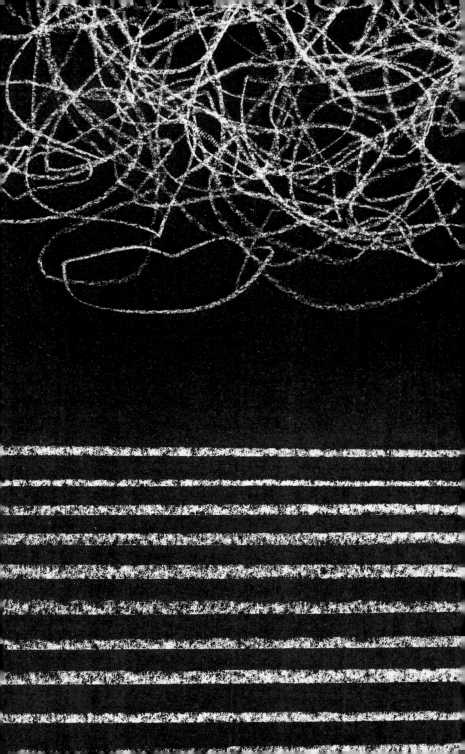

GOOD DOG

CALLIE

CHARLIE AND TOBY WERE BEST FRIENDS. Toby was our dog. Well, Toby was really Charlie's dog. For Charlie, Toby was everything humans aren't. Toby never rolled his eyes when he saw Charlie coming. Toby didn't care what my brother smelled like. Toby never asked Charlie to bring money to school for pizza. And not once did Toby ask my brother to make a list about showering and hair.

We got Toby when Charlie and I were seven. Mom read someplace that dogs can help kids with autism "become more verbal"—that a pooch can bring out the best in people like Charlie by encouraging them to speak, and that dogs can teach unconditional love and a whole lot of other good things.

I never read any of the books Mom did about dogs and kids with autism. I didn't need to read about the good things dogs could do because I saw it happening. Charlie loved Toby, and that big hairy Saint Bernard with the slobbery tongue loved my brother right back. From the time Toby was a puppy, he'd sleep in Charlie's bed. He didn't want to be anywhere else. I would even bring dog biscuits into my room to try and tempt Toby to hang out more with me, but those biscuits didn't cut it—Toby and Charlie were like macaroni and cheese. One couldn't exist without the other.

But sometimes even mac and cheese doesn't stick together in the right way. Things with Charlie and Toby weren't always perfect. Charlie had to work really hard to learn how to care for Toby. I remember getting so tired of reminding Charlie what had to be done for Toby each morning before we left for school.

Back then was when Mom was first trying to stop reminding (nagging) us about Toby's needs so that we would learn about the responsibility of having a dog. So, of course, I swooped in on Charlie and told him we had to make a chart of what needed to be done, and when.

Looking back, I remember how into it Charlie was. We sat down together at the kitchen table to make the chart while Mom prepped dinner. Mom acted like she wasn't paying attention, but Charlie and I knew good and well that while she chopped onions, she also listened to every word we said. I was the chart writer. Charlie drew super-straight lines for the chart.

We talked about what would make Toby the happiest and the safest when it came to eating, sleeping, playing, and bathing. We agreed that Toby deserved the same consideration we give to people. Charlie added that if he has chores, maybe Toby should, too. I thought Charlie was kidding, but he wasn't. To Charlie's way of thinking, everything had to be fair, even for pets.

But what kinds of chores could a dog do? The only thing we came up with was to make Toby listen to us read our homework out loud. We nixed that chore when we thought about how hard it would be to actually make a dog sit still and listen to us read. But the image of Toby sitting there with his tongue hanging out while we read from our schoolbooks really cracked us up. Even now, when we talk about it, we bust out laughing. That's one of the reasons Toby was so special. He made us laugh together.

Because Charlie takes things so literally, we had to spell out everything on the chart. And we bullet-pointed the list to make it even clearer. To most people, some of the stuff would be super obvious, but not always with Charlie.

The chart for Monday said:

- *Let Toby out as soon as you wake up.*
- *Let Toby back in.*
- *Feed Toby breakfast.*
- *Keep Toby inside when leaving for school.*
- *When you get home from school, let Toby out.*
- *Play with Toby for twenty minutes outside, longer if you both want.*
- *Feed Toby his dinner right before we sit down for our dinner.*

- *Let Toby out again.*
- *Let Toby back inside.*
- *Let Toby out one more time before you go to bed.*
- *Clean up Toby's poop in the yard.*
- *Remember to let Toby in.*

Most days would be the same, but some days, instead of *play*, we wrote *walk*. Other days, we included treats for Toby. And once a week, we added that Toby needs a bath.

The chart was like a road map for Charlie. He was awesome at following it, and did a great job with his new best friend, Toby.

Their friendship grew and grew and grew. Charlie and Toby were better than mac and cheese together—they were cake with icing. Like a cake (well, gluten-free cake for us), together they were sweet and made people smile.

But then last year, Toby started to run slower and he didn't seem to want to eat. One day when I was petting Toby, I felt a big bump by his left ear. Charlie felt it, too.

Then we did something that made the whole thing worse—we went on the Internet and typed in "bump on dog's ear." Why did we do that? The minute you type in "bump" and "dog," the whole computer screen goes crazy and starts throwing medical reports at you! Every single one said "tumor." And they all seemed to say that what Toby had was serious.

Mom and Dad let us miss school to go with Toby to the vet. What a crazy scene. There were so many noisy animals in the waiting room. The vet must've been having a special on bird checkups—so much squawking! It drove Charlie crazy. He kept biting his lip and twisting Toby's collar in his hands, alternating the collar with the strings from his hoodie. I tried not to make it worse by talking too much. Charlie looked straight ahead and didn't say a word.

Finally, Toby's name was called. Charlie was slow to come, but he did as we made our way silently to a big room in the back. The vet was a kind-looking woman with big brown eyes. She asked Charlie's permission to touch Toby. Charlie nodded, but he kept looking at the floor. The vet confirmed what we'd found online—Toby had a tumor and was very sick with cancer. We had three options: surgery, chemo-therapy, or what she called comfort care. To this day, I don't know what she meant by "comfort care," but Charlie seemed to understand somehow. He nodded every time she talked about making Toby comfortable.

I kept wondering, *How can a dog be comfortable if he's dying? And how can the kids who love that dog be comfortable when that dog is dying?*

Either way, the vet told us that Toby didn't have much longer to live. We left the office silently, and didn't say a word the whole way home in the car.

At dinner that night, Charlie told Cole and Chris about Toby. My brother, the kid who struggles to get his words together and his thoughts out clearly, made a case quietly and methodically for comfort care. He could've been a lawyer defending Toby's right to feel good in his final days. None of us could argue with Charlie. It was one of the few times I've seen him express such a passionate, clear opinion.

And there was more. Charlie talked about not

wanting to "fix" anyone with treatments and surgeries. That sometimes things that were meant to be just were.

After that, we all started to spoil Toby. Charlie and I made a new chart, which included lots of playtime, dog treats, and major cuddles.

Toby only lived a few more months. The final weeks were really hard on all of us, especially Charlie. What do you say to your twin brother when his best friend is dying? What do you tell your brother with autism about life and death, when all he can see is that the dog he loves is leaving his life forever? When I think about it now, I realize that there's nothing you can say in that situation to make it better.

Being a twin, I could really feel Charlie's confusion and pain. I could feel *his* heart breaking in *my* heart. Is that part of the beauty of being a twin? I ask myself this all the time.

During Toby's decline, Charlie, who has always been hyperaware of what was fair, talked and talked about Toby's disease not being fair.

When Toby died, Charlie stopped talking to the family. He didn't even get excited to play his video games. We just kept hearing the same few songs loop over and over again, coming out of his bedroom.

We gave Charlie space to heal. I sat in his room a lot, silent, hoping Charlie would talk to me about what he was feeling. It was stupid of me, I know. He hardly ever talks about his true feelings, because he often doesn't have the right words to describe them. Instead, we just listened to the same three songs. Until one day, Charlie added new songs to the mix, and that's when I knew he was starting to heal.

We haven't gotten a new dog yet. We're taking it slow. I'm hoping that the next one will be as good a friend to Charlie as Toby was, but can also be bribed to my bedroom with biscuits.

CHARLIE

TOBY.

My best friend.

Never coming back.

· Still miss him.

Do I want another dog?

Not yet.

That's all I have to say about Toby.

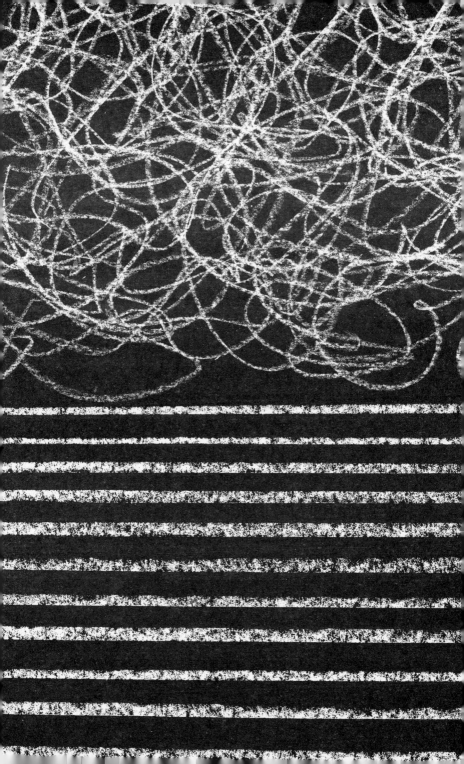

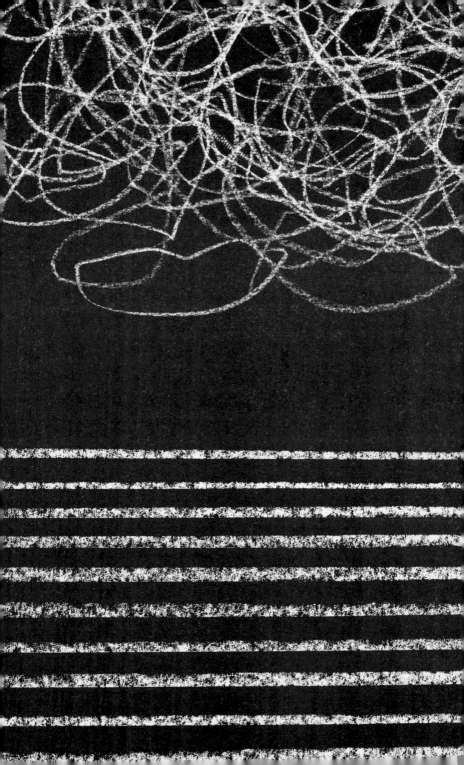

A FULL PLATE

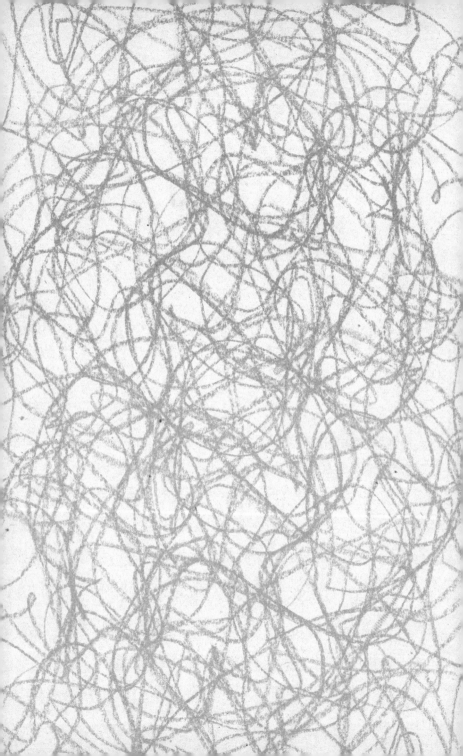

CHARLIE

THIS MORNING, MOM ASKED ME WHAT I WANTED FOR DINNER.

I told her I don't know.

She told me to think about it.

Why does everyone want me to think about things?

I'm sick of thinking.

Thinking makes my head hurt.

What's so good about thinking?

CALLIE

DINNERTIME CAN GO ONE OF TWO WAYS—OKAY OR HORRIBLE.

When Charlie and I get home from school, he seems good—happy, and not totally exhausted or frustrated by his day.

Step One to an Okay Dinner.

We finish our homework without a lot of drama, even though Dad and Charlie have their nightly tug-of-war about him doing his homework with music on. This evening, there's an added argument about Charlie's English paper when Dad tells Charlie to "think about what you're saying" in his essay.

Charlie shoots back, "No, no, no!"

And we've now dropped to Step Negative One to an Okay Dinner. If Dad pushes too much, Charlie will melt down into a tantrum. He'll bring his melted-down self to the dinner table, and I can forget about enjoying my food since we'll all be trying to calm you-know-who.

Will Dad ever learn that English is torture for Charlie, and that if it was as simple as "think about what you're saying," Charlie wouldn't be the kid he is?

But okay, the argument doesn't escalate, and we're good for the moment.

Back on Step One to an Okay Dinner. Charlie's calm. I'm calm. *Please, God, make it last.*

Mom calls us to eat. When we get downstairs, no one looks up from what they're doing. Cole and Chris are huddled over their textbooks. My parents are in the kitchen, pulling together the dinner fixings before we all sit down.

As soon as I see that we're having homemade pizza, and that each of us will get to pick our toppings, we're onto Step Two to an Okay Dinner: Serve something Charlie loves.

Since we're now gluten free (GF, as we call it), Mom has set out the GF pizza dough, which I can tolerate when it's covered with our favorite toppings. We have an assembly line of goodies to put on our pizzas, which takes us up to Step Two and a Half to an Okay Dinner.

No complaints from anyone, because we can all pick what we want. Pizza dinner night is also fun because we make it into a game to see who can remember which toppings everyone's chosen. Charlie and I always make the exact same concoction—pepperoni, banana pepper, and bell pepper special, with tons of cheese. Mom, Dad, and our brothers always choose something different, so part of the game involves having a good memory.

As soon as our crusts are piled high with what we love, Charlie is happy and smiling, and kidding around with me, Chris, and Cole. That takes us up all the way to Step Four to an Okay Dinner.

Soon it's time for the game. Who can remember all the toppings for each person? The winner gets the first serving of dessert. We don't even bother getting a pen and paper—Charlie can always remember all of the toppings! He's like a pizza encyclopedia.

But tonight, Dad and Charlie are neck and neck with their pizza-toppings memory. I can see Charlie getting agitated. He hates to lose this game. *Oh no, here it comes*, I think. *Meltdown central.*

I start bumping down the steps to an Okay Dinner faster than a little girl tripping on a flight of stairs in six-inch heels—*Clunk! Clunk! Clunk! Clunk!*

I'm almost to the bottom, ready to land on my butt, and feeling disappointment, when Dad says he's out of the game and is passing his win over to Charlie.

Dad thinks this is a good idea, but I'm thinking, *Noooo, Dad!*

This will make it worse, not better. Charlie's gonna think he's being babied. He'll start yelling, push his chair back from the table, and stomp to his room. I'm now on the bottom of the Okay Dinner Steps. My mind fast-forwards and hears Charlie's music pounding through the house, and my stomach tensing as it churns to digest the peppers and cheese.

But, by a miracle, nothing happens. Charlie breaks into a grin, tells Dad it isn't fair to back out of a game.

Huge relief.

But we're not safe yet. All Dad needs to do is mention Charlie's English paper, and the whole night will crumble.

I wait. I pray. I let the peppers and cheese settle in my stomach.

Charlie says, "I get dessert first. Bring on the ice cream."

He scoops a big hunk of chocolate from the container.

When it's my turn to get dessert, I let the sweet cream drip down my throat, thankful.

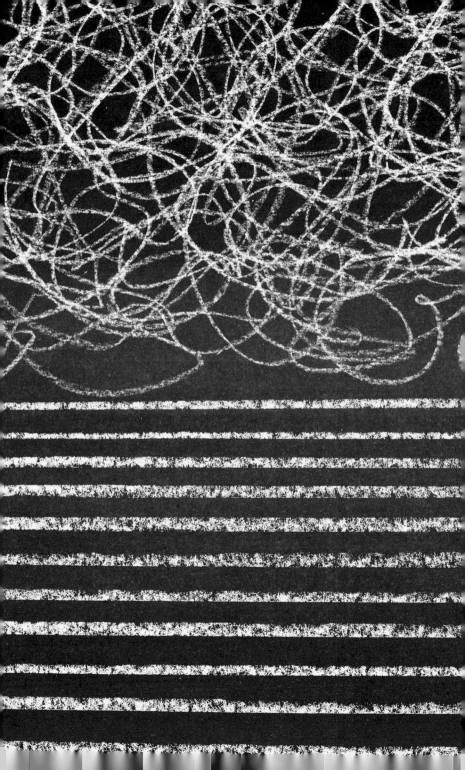

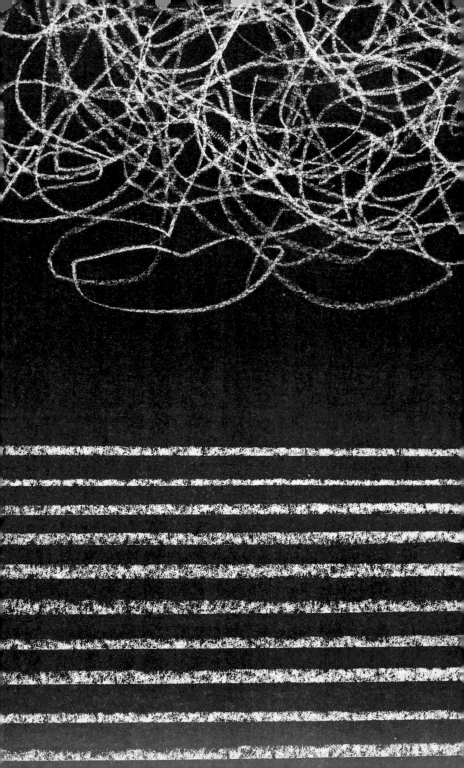

ARE WE
THERE YET?

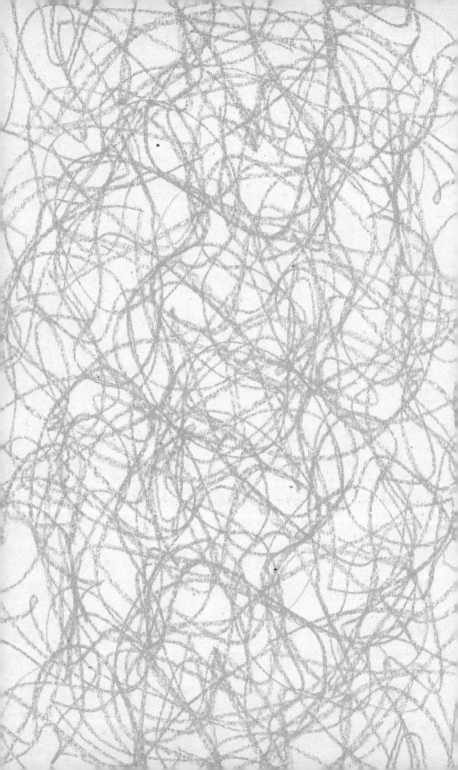

CHARLIE

HOW DID WE GET TO DECEMBER ALREADY? I don't care how we got here. We're here, and that means it's time to kick back and go on our family vacation.

I love vacations.

And I hate vacations.

And I love vacations.

And I hate them.

I love swimming in a pool.

I hate airports.

I love being out in the sun all day.

I hate airplane rides.

I love sweet drinks that are served in hollowed-out pineapples with little paper umbrellas sticking out the top.

I hate restaurants.

I love having no school.

Why are there so many drink choices from those people who bring you drinks on the airplane?

Can you bring a dog on a plane?

Why didn't anyone ever tell me you could bring a dog on a plane?

Would Toby have liked a ride on a plane?

Is Toby in the sky where the plane will be?

Will I see Toby?

CALLIE

THERE ARE EXACTLY NINETY-SEVEN DAYS FROM THE FIRST DAY OF SCHOOL TO HOLIDAY BREAK. I've been counting. Finally, finally, we're here, on our way to the Caribbean.

But it's not as simple as that. When your brother has autism, you don't just go on vacation. You fight your way past your brother's issues and struggle through every step to what makes you feel that you need a vacation to get over the "vacation" of spending a week with Charlie.

So here we are, on our way. Charlie is moving slower than slow as people shove to get through airport security. His hoodie's hood is pulled tight. He's twisting its strings, trying to avoid the loud sounds and harsh airport lights that are coming in and down and all around.

We're on "Charlie time." That means none of us can rush or even think about moving fast, even though everyone around us is hurrying and shoving to get to their vacations. If we try to rush Charlie, he gets agitated, and our vacation is over before we even get started. We have to be at the airport three hours before any flight we take to allow Charlie more time.

To help calm himself down, Charlie talks to everyone in every line—at the security checkpoints, at the snack store, at the airplane gate. And in each line, he asks people if he can go ahead of them.

At every turn, Mom and Dad look frazzled. Chris and Cole are beyond annoyed, and are slapping at each other and acting up.

I'm the calm one, explaining to Charlie what's going on and helping him stay on track. I wish I could slap at someone. Or I wish someone would slap at me. At least that would give me a reason to slap back, which is how I'm feeling inside.

But hey, I want this vacation. I need it. So I'll do whatever it takes to keep it together. We're not even on the plane yet. I want to get on that plane! I want to lift up past the clouds, into a place where the sky is below me. I want to, for just a few hours, be above the world.

At the gate, there's more Charlie to handle. He asks questions about everything. He's impatient. He has trouble waiting. He's antsy. Always antsy.

He wants to know:

Why can't we get on the plane right now?

Why do we have to wait for our turn to board?

What's that noise over there?

Does that lady have a dog in her bag?

Can dogs go on planes?

Can I pet the dog?

What is the dog's name?

With Charlie moving slow, slow, and more slow in the plane's aisle—where he's blocking people who are less than happy that my six-foot-tall, size-twelve-feet brother is taking his own sweet time—we finally settle into our seats for the five-hour trip. Charlie's obsessed with having a window seat. He flips if he doesn't get one.

The pilot asks that we turn off all electronic devices. For Charlie, that's like asking him to turn off his brain. He loves his iPad. Its puzzles and games keep him distracted and calm. He won't shut the thing off until the flight attendant insists. Of course, Charlie has to ask *why, why, why,* and *when, when, when* can he turn it back on. And *what, what, what* is he supposed to do now? The flight attendant tries to explain, tries to break it down for Charlie, who is sitting next to me. "I'll take care of it," I tell her, and she moves on while I gently coax the iPad from Charlie.

The plane takes off. So do I. In my mind, I'm soaring. Climbing. High and higher. I don't think there's a place high enough for me. There's no way to truly escape my all-the-time-eye-on-Charlie, but at least I can close my eyes and imagine the beach that will soon greet us.

I'm really enjoying my dream-meditation, when the flight attendant shows up with the beverage cart. She asks Charlie what he wants to drink. He has her list all the available sodas and juices. He asks her to repeat the list—four times. I've got one eye open. My beach meditation is long gone. Charlie's getting overwhelmed. He's squeezing his hands together. He's kicking the seat in front of him. He starts to ask for the beverage list a fifth time, but then settles on water.

I sink low into my seat. I should have talked to Charlie about all the drink options as soon as we got on the plane, or I should have just ordered for him. But I can't plan for every little crisis that might happen. I'm so sick of this. I can't manage every single blip that pops up on *The Charlie Show*.

Pretty soon the seat belt sign goes off and we're smooth sailing. I tell Charlie that even though the sign is off, he still has to keep the seat belt on. He looks confused but doesn't argue, especially because Mom and Dad's credit card is making its way around so all four of us can watch whatever movie we want. I take out some snacks, Charlie does the same, and all of us relax. Finally.

I sleep deeply. I can even feel myself snoring, but don't care. I'm woken with a start when Charlie begins hitting my arm. He's been watching the virtual map for hours and knows exactly how much longer we have left. The good news is that we're halfway there. The bad news is that we're only halfway there.

"We'll arrive soon," I tell him.

Charlie sees that the seat belt sign is currently not lit up, and he can't sit still any longer. He gets out of his seat to explore. Like a rocket, I go after him. He glares at me, but I tell him I need another drink and ask him if he wants to come with me. We quickly make our way to the flight attendant. I order for both of us this time. We carefully walk back to our seats with our drinks. Meltdown averted.

When the pilot announces that we're about to land, I'm exhausted, but happy to be able to tell Charlie that we've arrived. He gets up out of his seat as if he's ready to walk off the plane, even though we're still flying. I have to tell him to sit down three times. He goes back to hitting my arm.

Next comes the ear popping. Another thing I forgot to mention to Charlie in advance. At least he thinks it's funny when we all hold our noses, puff our cheeks, and make monkey faces.

We land. The plane taxis to the gate. Charlie asks a million more questions. The doors open, and—*schwoop*—Charlie races off the plane, cutting in front of everyone in line. He starts running out of the terminal. We all run after him. We can't lose him now. I've waited too long for this. As I sprint, I've got my eyes on Charlie the whole time. People are pointing and gasping. I start calling—"Charlie!"

Thank goodness I'm a fast runner. When I catch up to him, I snatch his arm. I'm panting like a dog in the desert. I'm using every bit of restraint I can to not scream at Charlie. I hold on to him until Mom and Dad and our brothers catch up to us. Mom looks frantic, like she's going to cry.

Dad looks hot-mad.

Cole and Chris think the whole thing is funny.

I feel like I've just finished a marathon.

At baggage claim, Charlie's staring at the rotating luggage belt as it makes its way around.

The next few hours are a blur. Suitcases. A rental car. Hotel check-in.

Before I know it, though, someone mentions snorkeling, and we're changing into swimsuits. *Whew! This* is the vacation I've been waiting for. Bring on the snorkel gear! Bluer-than-blue ocean, here I come.

But wait—*what?*

Mom's saying something about heading to the pool for our snorkel session.

The pool? I did not get on a plane for five hours to snorkel in a *pool*!

But—*Charlie* needs that, Mom tells us.

No one is really sure how Charlie's going to feel about having a snorkel mask on his face, so my parents insist that we have a snorkel practice session in the hotel pool. And I am now one of those weird people who doesn't snorkel in the beautiful Caribbean Sea, but who flaps around with my fins in a pool where there are babies in floaties and old people doing the sidestroke. I have counted down ninety-seven days from September to now, for this.

And can I also say that just because Charlie needs to practice something doesn't mean we *all* need to practice something? But of course I don't say that. I just keep trying to be the perfect twin.

I jump into the pool with Charlie and grab our snorkeling gear. Charlie's a great swimmer. But we quickly learn that swimming and snorkeling are very different, mostly because of the equipment required. Charlie understands goggles, but something that restricts his breathing? Not so much. The snorkel mask is a brand-new experience for Charlie.

Another thing I wish I'd remembered to practice at home! We should've had Charlie wear the mask around the house. He hates all the gear. He keeps sucking in the water and choking.

The pool lifeguard, a pretty girl with freckles, comes over to see what's going on. She's smiling and gently helping Charlie, who is completely thrown into a lovey-dovey tailspin. He thinks the lifeguard has a crush on him! He's staring and staring at her. He starts trying to talk to her, but too much. He's asking all kinds of questions. And too much of those, too.

Then Charlie starts to awkwardly try and hold the lifeguard's hand and swing it back and forth. He has no idea that she's just being a friendly, polite lifeguard who is doing her job of keeping people safe at a pool, and does not want to hold hands with him, all girlfriend-boyfriend lovey-dovey.

I catch her eye and mouth *autism*. She winks at me, brushes over Charlie's awkward stares and chattering, and starts teaching him how to snorkel. This lifeguard is amazing—a gift from the god of vacations. She's super patient, and soon Charlie's snorkeling in the pool. We make plans to go in the ocean tomorrow. On the way back to our room, Charlie can't stop talking about the lifeguard.

Dinner at the resort is absolutely horrible. It's not the food that's bad—it's Charlie's behavior in public. He wants pizza. There's none on the menu. But he wants it. And he keeps asking the waiter for it. And she keeps telling him there's no pizza. And he keeps asking, and asking, and asking.

And he doesn't like sitting too long at the table.

And he refuses to read the menu or use new forks or knives.

And he worries about where the bathroom is.

And people are gawking at us.

And some people get up and leave.

And I want to get up and leave with them.

The only people in the place who aren't bothered by Charlie are toddlers. That's probably because my teenage brother is like a toddler. A tall toddler who has tall tantrums. Mom and Dad and I try to calm Charlie down, but we can't.

I manage to scarf down a salad, but I've lost my appetite.

The next morning, we wake up bright and early. I'm bouncing with excitement. Charlie doesn't take time to feel or look at anything. He forges ahead, puts on his snorkel gear, motions for me to join him. We head out first, before the rest of the family.

I relish the feeling of the sand on my toes as I look out into the calm, clear water. *Yes! Yes! Yes! At last!*

Charlie quickly gets to waist-deep in the water. He immediately grips my hand like he did when we were little kids. Bit by bit, we both kick gently into the ocean's blue wonder, pointing out yellow fish and coral, and seaweed.

We spend the entire day snorkeling.

It is magical.

And beautiful.

And quiet.

Charlie and me, floating.

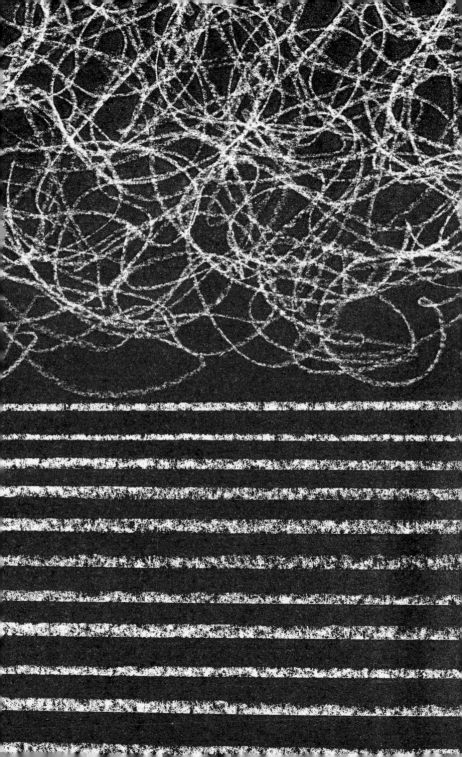

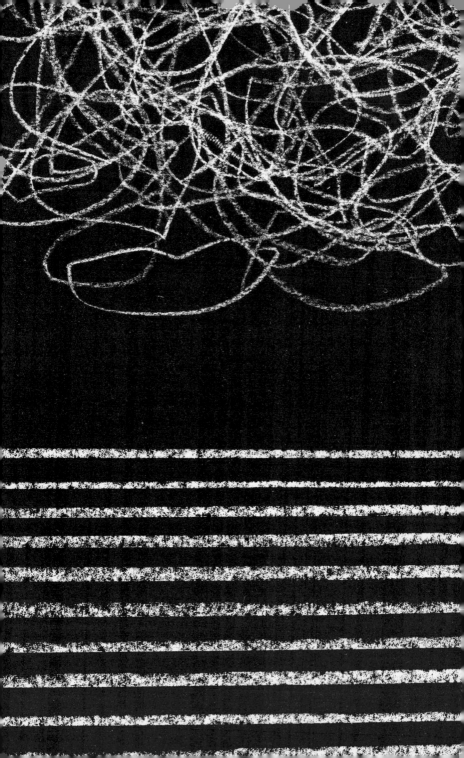

HAPPY BIRTHDAY
TO WHO?

CALLIE

TWIN BIRTHDAYS ARE DOUBLE THE FUN. And double the not-fun.

We get two of everything.

Every year, my family sings "Happy Birthday" twice. Since Charlie is two minutes older, we sing his name first. It's a good thing my brother came into this world before I did. That way, he doesn't have to wait to hear his name inserted into the birthday song.

We like to sing loudly. When we get to *"Happy biiiirthday, dear Charlie"* (the loudest part), Charlie's hands clamp over his ears, and he begs us to stop.

When my turn comes—*"Happy biiiirthday, dear Callie"*—I'm all about celebrating. But my family's singing volume has been turned way down so that Charlie's ears won't hurt. Hearing your name whispered in "Happy Birthday" is like having a celebration for a newborn who's taking a nap. When I hear it, I'm thinking, *Thanks for the lullaby.*

As always, we have two cakes and two sets of candles. This year, there are sixteen candles on each cake. That's a lot of blowing out and wishing. Charlie blows on his candles first, real hard, spit flying from his mouth. He starts to tell everyone his wish. He does this every year. And every year, we shush him before he can blurt it out.

Chris says, "Your wish won't come true if you say it, Charlie, remember?"

Cole says, "You can tell me your wish later, and I'll hold on to it for you."

This is supposed to be our sweet sixteenth year, but something about it feels stale.

When it's my turn to blow out the candles, I do it one candle at a time, wishing silently on each:

1. I wish *"Happy biiiirthday, dear Callie"* could be sung at the top of our lungs.
2. I wish my nails would grow.
3. I wish I had a boyfriend.
4. I wish Mom and Dad would let me have a boyfriend.
5. I sometimes wish I weren't a twin.
6. I wish they would invent gluten-free birthday cake that tastes like real cake.
7. I wish Charlie was a normal brother.
8. I wish I had a sister.
9. I wish I had only sisters.
10. I wish I didn't have a math test tomorrow.
11. I wish Charlie hadn't gotten autism.
12. I wish to go to college someday.
13. I wish to win a Grammy for Best New Artist.
14. I wish the boyfriend I'm wishing for turns out to be Kadir Collier, from my homeroom.
15. I wish my parents could see me better.
16. I wish I had more wishes.

CHARLIE

COLE WANTS ME TO TELL HIM MY BIRTHDAY WISH.

"Too late," I say. "You could've heard it before, but everybody shut me up."

What none of my family knows is that I've put my blown-out candles under my pillow. Maybe that will make my wish come true.

All night long, I dream about Toby and me, playing, running, flying on a plane.

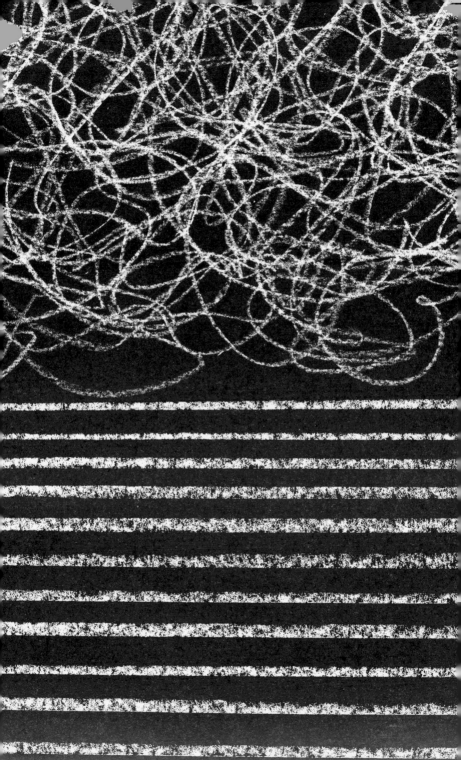

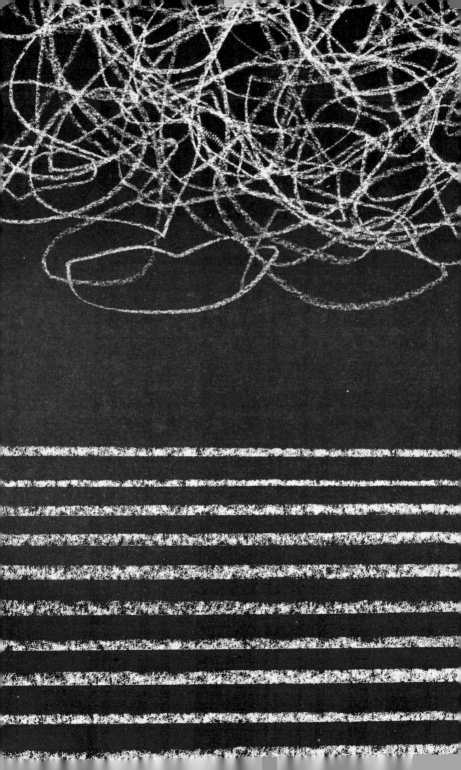

HELICOPTER PARENTS

CALLIE

MOM AND DAD ARE TWO LOW-FLYING CHOPPERS WHEN IT COMES TO SOCIAL MEDIA. Whenever Mom tells me that she and Dad used to pass handwritten notes back and forth to talk to each other in class, it's like a goofy scene from some old-time movie—it's so throwback. Kids do still write notes in school, but only sometimes.

Anyway, my parents, who grew up in the Dark Ages of notes in class, stalk me on Facebook and

Instagram. It's ten times worse for Charlie. Mom and Dad are always waging an assault on my brother's social media stuff, and lecturing us about why it's important to keep Charlie safe in cyberspace, which Dad calls a town without a sheriff.

It's so confusing for Charlie why he can't post what he wants, when he wants. He wishes he could express himself like every other teenager. He asks me constantly.

Why can't *I say what I want?*

How come Mom and Dad have to look at it?

What's bad that could happen?

Who cares what I'm doing on Facebook?

Where is there a rule book?

I try to explain it to him, but it's not easy. I carefully tell him about a girl in my class whose sister posted an inappropriate video of her saying curse words. When a college saw this, they took back their acceptance.

"But she didn't say the curse words to the college people," Charlie reasons.

I keep working to explain. "She didn't need to say it right to them. When you put something on social media, you *do* say it to anyone who's watching or reading."

Charlie doesn't fully get it, so I give another example that he might be able to understand. I tell him about when a young unarmed teen was shot by police, the news media used his negative posts against him to hurt his character. It's complicated, and I can see by the way Charlie's looking off that he's not taking it in or comprehending.

Like everything else, Charlie sees social media in black and white. It's one way or the other. But there's a lot of in-between on Twitter and Instagram and Facebook. Charlie can think he's saying one thing but really sound like he means something else. Or somebody bad could message Charlie and encourage him to do something dangerous, and he wouldn't have a clue. It's worse than when Charlie was tricked into showing up with the fifty dollars for pizza. And it's why my parents stalk us—because they don't want someone evil to stalk us.

I tell Charlie all of this, yet he still makes a big mistake. One night before dinner, I hear Mom and

Charlie in a conversation that's on fire and is coming from Charlie's bedroom. He's posted "Autism can suck it!" on Twitter, and Mom has shut down his account.

Charlie is slamming at the wall. Mom's heated words are slamming at Charlie.

He doesn't speak to anyone in the house for a week. It's radio silence on *The Charlie Show*. When your brother has autism, radio silence is a bad signal. When your brother retreats into his own world, there's no calling him back until he's ready. Like when Toby died.

But still, I try and try, and always try. As much as I wish *The Charlie Show* would go on hiatus more often, I get scared when Charlie becomes nonverbal. After days and nights of no-talk Charlie, I finally make him giggle by telling him I laughed when I read his post, and so did my friends. Charlie really starts to crack up when I let him know that before Mom made him delete his post, it got a ton of *Like*s.

CHARLIE

MOM AND DAD ARE ALWAYS TELLING ME TO TELL THE TRUTH. So I did. On Twitter. The truth is, autism *does* suck.

It's because of sucky autism that I can't post whatever I want like every other teenager I know. When I posted that message, I was mostly mad at autism and wasn't telling anyone that they suck, so nobody should've cared or been offended.

But I can't post anything on social media without the Social Media CIA (SM-CIA) watching me. My

Twitter or Instagram posts go directly to my parents' phones. Once when I posted about how much I love Jillian, three seconds later, I got a "please delete that last post" message from the SM-CIA.

I was so mad that I shot back another post. It was meant to be a joke, but the SM-CIA didn't think it was funny.

I put the middle finger up on Instagram. That forced us into having a two-hour "family summit."

During the summit, I asked, "So because I have autism, I gotta be watched for this, too?"

Together, at the same time, Dad and Mom said, "Yes."

I left the summit, went to my room, slammed the door, and put my middle finger up at the SM-CIA.

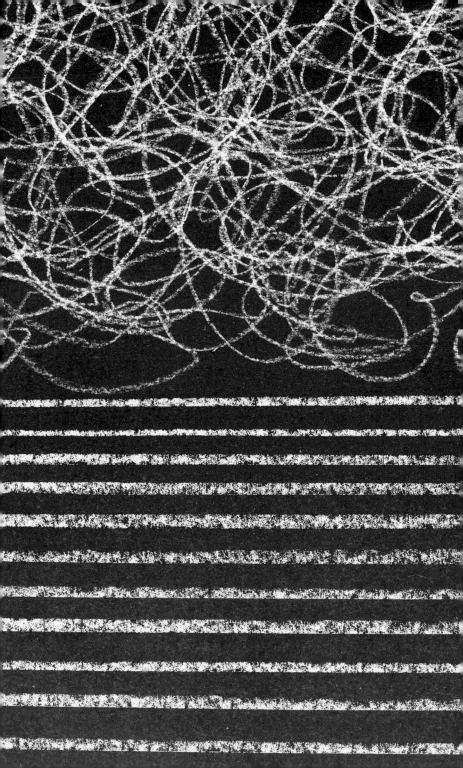

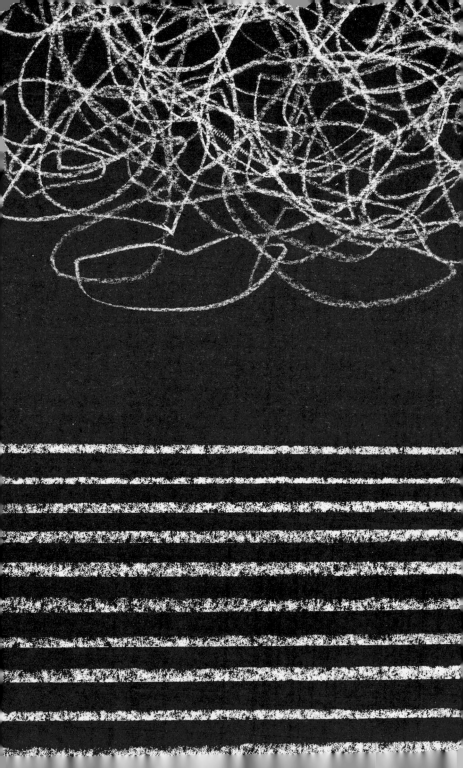

TRACK JOY, FOOTBALL HATE

CALLIE

WHEN SPRING COMES, FLOWERS SHOW UP IN GREEN GRASS.

Everything's new.

Somehow, *I am*, too.

Maybe it's the sunlight. Or the promise of longer days. Or the birds on my bedroom windowsill.

Spring also brings track season, and that's when I shine the brightest. Just like the flowers. Just like the sun.

When I run, I'm as happy as the birds who sing all day long.

When I run, the world blurs by me. The wind whips through my braids. The sun streaks across my face. I push myself harder and harder. For me, running track is joy, and freedom, and Callie time.

Mom tells me I started running before I was a year old and haven't stopped since. I joined track as soon as I started middle school. I knew I wanted to be part of a team. Part of a group that lets me just *be*. Part of something Charlie wasn't part of.

At school, track is all mine. It's all mine. The break-free ache that races through my whole body when I'm working every muscle in my legs, and feeling the air fill my lungs, is something no one can truly understand or take from me. My family knows this, and they let me have it. It's why I'm able to stay as late as I need to after school for track practice.

Today when practice ends, I'm too out of breath to speak with my teammates. We've been doing sprints to get ready for this week's race, and we're all pushing ourselves to the limit. The track meet is against our biggest rival, Billington High, so we need to be ready—*I* need to be ready. I love being out of breath. It means I need to slow down, to be quiet, to check in with myself. It means I need to feel my own heart beating. It means I need to listen to thoughts that rise up in my mind as my breathing comes back to me.

People talk a lot about "catching your breath." After a hard run, it's like my breath is catching me. It's like my soul is tapping me on the shoulder, and saying, *Callie, here I am. Take a moment to feel my presence.*

So I let my breath—my soul and heart's voices— catch me.

Later, at home, even the stupidest junk coming from Chris, Cole, or Charlie doesn't bother me one bit. On a night after track practice, Mom and Dad can nag me about whatever, and I'm cool with it. That's track's gift. It's what getting in touch with what "catches me" does.

On the day of our track meet, my family comes out to cheer me and my team. With three brothers and both parents on the scene, my family makes up a rowdy cheering section. I love them for this. And I love hearing my name chanted by the people I love, who also annoy me because they love to clap and scream and call out to me when I'm not running.

That's my family, who's also shown up with DayGlo signs that say:

Callie, you GO, girl!

and

Kill it, Callie!

and

Callie's Got Speed!

Charlie always comes to my meets, but he's no cheerleader. These things are hard for him. There are lots of people he doesn't know, crazy cymbal and bull-horn sounds, screaming, nonstop motion, and crowd chaos. It's strange, though. As much as all of this noise and squalor grate on Charlie in most situations, my track meets are one of the few loud, frenzied places where Charlie doesn't do anything that might embarrass me.

He watches closely. Hands in his lap, but never once covering his ears or in his pants. Charlie even endures the starter pistol's *pop!* that goes off each time a new heat begins.

In today's competition, we're closely tied with Billington High. The final relay will cinch it for us—or for them. My coach, Ms. Davis, lets me know that

I'll be doing the final leg of the deciding relay. Marcy. Becker will hand off the baton to me, and I'm the one who's got to make it to the finish line.

I'm completely stoked. So is my team. My family and school and everybody at the meet are in an all-out hyper hollering party whose pitch is shrill. I breathe deeply. I'm practically shoving air into my lungs each time I inhale. On the exhales, I'm pushing that air out harder than hard. As soon as I see Marcy approaching, I start in with my feet, jogging to get momentum. Then—*thwack!*—the baton smacks my palm, and I'm flying. I can see Billington's runner at my shoulder. She's fast, but I'm faster—or so I think. That girl starts to gain on me, and is now inches ahead. My lungs burn with the scorch of intense breathing.

That's when I hear it—*Callie, here I am. Take a moment to feel my presence.*

The finish line is a yellow blur of plastic tape, pulling me to its power.

I lunge. Forehead forward. Chest pressed into the bright tape blur.

I am the winner!

CHARLIE

MY SISTER RUNS SO FAST.

What is she running to?

Who is she running from?

I don't know the answers. But I do know I feel pride when she wins.

Yes, we are twins. Same but different.

When Callie does track, something quiet happens inside me, from watching her. Seeing her go, seeing her so happy, somehow makes me happy, too.

But sports and me, we don't mix. We can't mix. I suck at being on a team.

I have tried it. I have hated it. I have hated every minute of every sport I've ever tried. That's because sports have:

1. People
2. Competition
3. Coordination
4. Away games or meets
5. Coaches who yell

There's another problem with sports. My dad was a professional football player who lives and breathes and believes in sports. Cole and Chris are like Dad—they're all about throwing a ball. And tackling each other. And being on the team.

Dad calls football a "man's sport."

I call football a headache.

Dad thinks that because I'm a good swimmer, I should also be a good football player. Doesn't he see the difference? Gliding in a pool at my own pace is nothing like getting creamed on a field.

But Dad insists that a sport is a sport is a sport. So

we practice football in our backyard once a week. Me, Callie, and our brothers. Even Callie's good at throwing and kicking. My sister can play a "man's sport" better than me.

I try to keep at it. Dad says we're Team Garrison and that I'm an important member. This gives me an idea—a football game that doesn't involve me *playing* football. Instead, I can participate in this man's sport by being the Stat Man. I can find out all kinds of football statistics and memorize them in ways not even Callie or Dad could do. We can have a family stat contest. Yeah, then we'll see who the real man is.

Everybody agrees to my idea. That night for dinner, Mom makes a special Football Stat Feast of wings, dips, and gluten-free chips.

I slap my cup on the table. "Order, order! It's time for Charlie's official football stat rules."

They're all paying attention. I let them know that the stat winner will be free of household chores for a whole week, even Mom and Dad. Everyone agrees.

That night, I'm up all hours on my laptop getting stats. I spend the next three nights getting more stats, until I'm so filled with football facts, nobody can tackle me. The information sticks in my brain like Krazy Glue. I couldn't unstick the stats if I tried.

My brothers *do* try.

They ask me about NFL receivers and quarterbacks. They want to know about catches, interceptions, sacks, and touchdowns. They drill me about games and Super Bowls from as far back as 1973. None of them can stump me! But I can stump—and trump—every member of Team Garrison.

As the week rolls on, I'm winning. By Friday, there's no contest. I'm the Stat Man, who will not be taking out the trash or emptying the dishwasher till next Friday.

My family's happy I've got them beat. Dad's the most excited. We have some of our best talks ever—about our NFL draft picks, Black Mondays, and bad ref calls.

Tonight at bedtime, Dad comes into my room. I'm on the computer gathering even more stats. It's inching onto midnight.

"Time to go to sleep, Charlie," Dad says.

"But, Dad, c'mon, I love this stuff," I say.

Dad says, "Charlie, I love *you*."

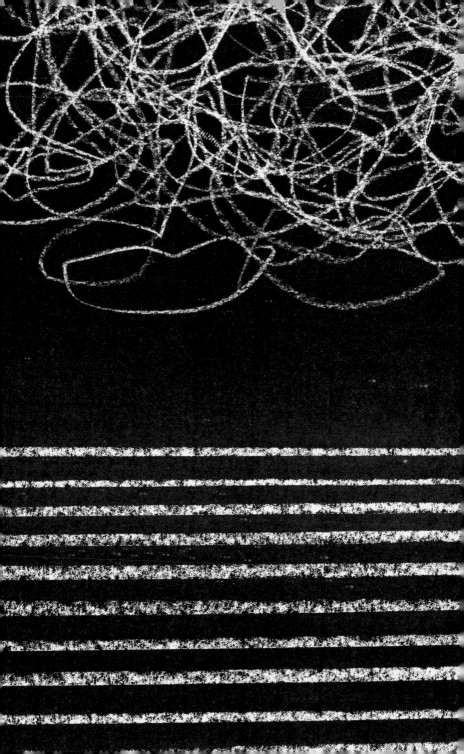

CHARLIE +
JILLIAN

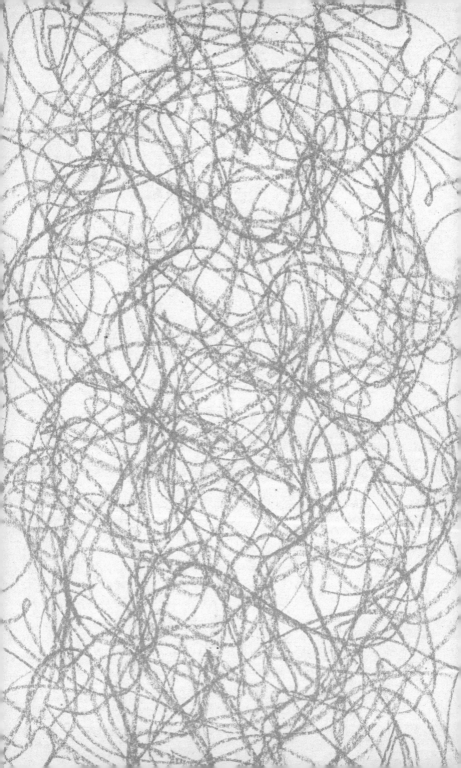

CHARLIE

DAD'S STILL COACHING ME. Not in football. But on how to get a girlfriend.

"You need to practice," he says.

He tells me it's the same as when you practice a football play, or when you study for a test, or rehearse lines for a play. I'm bad at all those things.

I'm not even good at talking to regular people I don't care about, so talking to a girl I like—that's beyond any kind of practicing. How can you practice not getting nervous, or having your neck sweat, or not mumbling, or keeping from looking at the ground? I admit, Dad's a good coach, but there's no way he can coach me out of stuttering, or forgetting what I want to say, or not remembering what I've just said, or getting so mixed up in a conversation that I'm repeating what I'm saying to remember what I'm saying, so I won't ever forget what I think I'm trying to say.

There's this girl, Jillian. She's awesome. Pretty, smart, has tons of friends, including Callie. Also, Jillian has known me since we were little. She really knows me. She never makes fun of me. To her, I'm like everyone else.

Justin and Steve don't think I stand a chance getting a date with Jillian. But I do. I know I do. At school, whenever she sees me in the halls, she smiles and waves. If I ask her for a date, she'll say yes. I just have to get the words out.

Practicing with Dad is no help. "Take it slow," he coaches.

I try. "Jillian, hi, I'm Charlie."

Dad is wringing his hands, like he's the one asking for the date.

I say, "Wait—I mean, no. I mean, Jillian already knows who I am."

Dad says, "Keep it simple. It's just a question. 'Would you like to go to the movies with me on Friday?'"

My voice cracks. "It's not just a question! It's Jillian."

I don't like this coaching. It feels worse than trying to catch a football.

I'm done with Dad. I don't even bother telling him this coaching thing is a waste of time. I go to my bedroom to practice in my mirror.

"Jillian, I'm Char—"

"Jillian, I like movies."

"Jillian, remember the time you came over when we were little, and there was a playdate . . . and . . . we . . . it was really fun . . . and—"

"Jillian, at the movies they have popcorn."

I want to punch the mirror. This is stupid. Practicing is making it worse.

The next day, I see Jillian in line at the school cafeteria. All the veins in my body are twisting around like licorice in a knot. I cut past kids in the line to get to Jillian. They're shoving me back and not liking that I'm cutting.

"Jillian—!" She looks startled.

"Hi, Charlie."

"My name is—"

Oh God, what is my name?

Oh God, she just said my name.

Oh God, Jillian has such a pretty name.

I blurt, "Wouldyougotothemovieswithmeon Friday?"

Jillian's balancing a tray of French fries and pudding. She takes a bite out of a fry. "Sure" is all she says.

I blink. I can't think of the next thing to say.

Out comes: "Wouldyougotothemovieswithmeon Friday?"

Now Jillian is blinking at me. "Yes, Charlie. I will go to the movies with you on Friday."

Friday arrives. We are at the movies. Callie's at the movies, too, with her friends. I'm sitting next to Jillian. The movie starts. I'm not watching the movie. I'm watching Jillian. I can't breathe. But I guess I *can* breathe, because I'm still alive. How can I be breathing, though, if my whole body feels like a bag of rocks glued to my seat?

Dad's coaching was dumb, but I all of a sudden remember something Dad said that might help. He told me to excuse myself and go to the bathroom if I feel uncomfortable. So I do. I run out of the theater to the bathroom. I take a few deep breaths to just make sure I can really, truly breathe. I wash my hands three times, take a few more deep breaths, and go back.

Callie catches my eye as I return to the theater. She holds up her popcorn and motions to eat it.

Oh crap. I forgot to buy Jillian any popcorn. What kind of boyfriend doesn't buy his girlfriend popcorn?

Callie is sitting on the other side of me. She whispers that maybe Jillian and I would like to share her popcorn. I grab the popcorn container from Callie, who rolls her eyes but says nothing. But I've snatched the popcorn too hard and the whole thing spills— onto Jillian. She brushes off the popcorn without even saying anything. She's really into this movie. Callie is sinking in her seat.

I only have to excuse myself one more time during the rest of the movie. After what seems like days have passed, the movie ends. I have no idea what the movie was about. I only remember that I'm still alive and can breathe, and that my hands are really clean from washing them in the bathroom so much.

The lights turn back on. Jillian looks over at me and smiles that pretty Jillian smile. I try to ask her what she thought of the movie, but instead I say, "How was the popcorn?"

I don't even wait for her answer because I don't want to get stuck in the line getting out the door.

I quickly weave my way through the people and somehow manage to meet up outside with Callie and Jillian and the other kids who've come with us to the movies.

Callie storms up to me, with Jillian next to her.

Callie asks, "Charlie, did you forget something?"

I check my pockets. Nope—I have my wallet, my gum, and my borrowed cell phone from Mom. "I'm good," I say.

"Are you sure?" Callie asks, motioning to Jillian.

Oh crap. Oh crap. Oh crap. Oh crap.

Yeah, I forgot something important—another one of Dad's coaching tips. Make sure I walk Jillian out of the theater.

I mumble, "Sorry."

Jillian takes my hand. "Don't apologize for being you," she says.

We walk toward the ice-cream parlor.

We're holding hands . . . We're holding hands . . . We're holding hands.

CALLIE

AN EMAIL TO CHARLIE THAT I WILL NEVER SEND, AND WILL DELETE AFTER I'VE WRITTEN IT.

TO: Charlie
FROM: Callie
RE: HUMILIATION!

Charlie:

I don't have the energy to even show my face

tomorrow. I have never felt so mortified. I wonder if you're feeling even an ounce of guilt right now.

I hope Jillian is willing to even look at me tomorrow.

Also—you are in no way ready for a girlfriend.

Okay, so you guys held hands. But if I hadn't been at the movies, would you have just left Jillian at the theater?

What were you thinking, Charlie?

Oh, excuse me, how could I forget?

You weren't thinking.

Are you ever thinking, Charlie?

Can you ever, for once, think right?!

No, you can't. That is impossible.

I know that's got to be hard.

I know you couldn't help it.

I know you weren't doing any of this to me.

So, okay, I will cut you some slack.

But it was still humiliating.

End of story.

DELETE!!

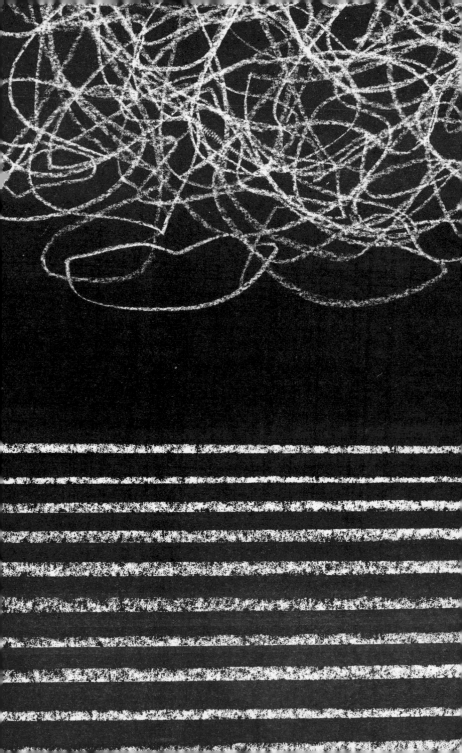

DANCE PRACTICE

CALLIE

A WEEK LATER, JILLIAN IS STILL MY BEST FRIEND.
Not once has she even mentioned *The Movie Disaster*.
Nobody else has brought it up, either. To them, it was
no big deal.

But is *this* really happening?

Jillian has invited Charlie to the Girl-Ask-Guy
dance at school.

Now I wonder if *Jillian* is thinking right!

Does she know what she's getting herself into?

Should I tell her Charlie doesn't dance?

He loves music and can explain the beat to you, but there's some sort of disconnect between the rhythm and his body. When the music plays, he gets lost in his own weird interpretive dance that is something from another planet. Anybody who dares to go to a dance with Charlie better be brave. I guess Jillian's got some kind of strange courage. Or an odd wish to become the most-made-fun-of girl in tenth grade.

What kind of friend am I to let Jillian go through with this? A dark movie theater, where everybody's mostly paying attention to the movie, is one thing. But a dance, where the whole school is watching? I want to warn Jillian that she's about to commit social suicide, but just as I'm about to call her on the phone, Charlie's in the doorway of my bedroom, asking me to teach him how to dance.

Oh no. Anything but that.

There's pleading in Charlie's eyes. "Please," he says.

"What music do you want?" I ask him, and without answering, he starts to play one of his favorite beats on his phone.

I begin by swaying side to side and doing a lame step-together, step-together. Charlie's trying to learn it, but even his step-together is a spastic mess.

"Callie, *tell* me the steps," Charlie says.

That's not a bad idea, since telling involves memorizing, which Charlie does well. We look on YouTube and find some dance videos that have verbal and visual instructions. This is like a magic cure for spastic.

Charlie watches closely. We play the videos six times. Charlie barely blinks. His eyes are fixed to YouTube. All of a sudden, something clicks, and my brother is dancing half decently.

He's not Usher or Justin Timberlake, and he's not even totally on the beat with the music. But if someone who didn't know Charlie were plunked down into this moment and saw his moves, they'd think the kid could sort of dance.

On the night of the dance, Dad's got our SUV ready. He's taken it to the car wash, so the seats are free of Cole's sticky juice spills and Chris's half-eaten chicken nuggets. When it's time to go, Charlie's waiting in the driver's seat. Ever since some kid in his special ed class said that people with autism can't drive, Charlie's been obsessed with being behind the wheel. That kid's comment lit a fire in Charlie. He's determined to get his license, and he's gotten to be an expert on all kinds of sports cars. He's most in love with Lamborghinis. When Dad comes to the car, dangling his keys, he kicks Charlie out of the front.

"Hey, Speed Racer, get in the backseat."

"Can I at least start the car?" Charlie asks.

Every time we're ready to go somewhere, Charlie's waiting in the driver's seat. By now, he knows Dad will tell him he's not allowed to turn on the ignition, so he doesn't ask twice.

CHARLIE

I'M QUIET IN THE CAR AS DAD DRIVES ME AND CALLIE TO THE DANCE.

Someday, I'll be the one driving. Just because I have autism doesn't mean I can't get my license. Callie better look out, because when I learn to drive, I know I'll be better at it than her. She doesn't even care about getting her license.

It's weird. Whenever I talk about driving, Dad looks really sad, like somebody's just told him bad news. So on the way to the dance, I don't talk about it.

In my mind, I'm going over the dance moves I learned on YouTube.

And say hi to Jillian when you see her, I tell myself.

As soon as we walk into the school gym, I want to go home. Callie's off in the ladies' room messing with her hair. As soon as she comes back, I'm going to tell her we need to leave.

There aren't many ninth graders here, but lots of tenth- and eleventh-grade kids, and even some seniors. Balloons and streamers are everywhere. And a strobe light. And music I've never heard before. I wish I could turn into one of the balloons so I could just pop and be a little piece of blue plastic that nobody notices.

I try to block the flickering strobe light by clamping my hands over my eyes. Someone comes up from behind. Puts hands over mine. The hands are soft. They make me feel safe. I gently take them down and put my own hands down, too. It's Jillian! She looks happy to see me. "Hi," I say. That's the beginning of something I don't know what to call. It's a good feeling. Saying hi to Jillian is a really good feeling.

The deejay starts playing one of the YouTube songs Callie and I practiced dancing to.

The balloons look nice to me now.

The strobe light is like a star over my head.

Jillian pulls me onto the dance floor.

The song switches to something I don't know. But somehow it doesn't matter.

Jillian's right here with me.

We're facing each other.

Holding both hands.

Making up our own dance, and laughing.

I'm here.

Now.

Me.

Happy.

Charlie.

NEW TERRITORY

A MOTHER'S HOPE

Almost every parent of a child with autism that I've met on our family's journey shares the same fears and hopes. We pray our teenagers will transition into adulthood with self-reliance, a safe place to live, a job with a compassionate employer. More than anything, we want to be assured that our kids will develop the ability to self-advocate, and that they'll find a trusted community.

I've stayed awake many nights, wondering how my socially awkward son will handle the first time a girl sends him mixed social messages, or rejects him outright. And I worry about the abiding impact having a sibling with autism has had on my daughter, Ryan Elizabeth, and our sons Roman and Robinson.

As RJ's mother, I have advocated myself down to a pulp since the day he was diagnosed with autism. It's an ongoing battle—not just for me alone, but for our entire family. We have firsthand experience as passengers on the Autism Express. It can be a wild ride, with sky-high peaks set against quick, unexpected plummets to places so low, I've despaired of ever getting out of the valley.

As the mom of a black son, the anxieties are compounded. In a societal climate where young men of color are perceived as threatening, I often worry that my hoodie-loving son (he has them folded and color coded in his closet) will find himself in a dangerous scenario that he can't correctly process and will end up physically hurt, or worse. And I often fear that his intentions will be misunderstood and that he'll pay an ugly price for that.

The issue of medication is one that we grapple with as well. As a parent, one of the most difficult challenges has been the decision to medicate or not to medicate. What drug? How much? What are the side effects? I want RJ to be RJ. I don't want to alter his personality. I love who he is, and I wouldn't change him for the world. (I would, however, try to change the world for him.)

I don't want to alter RJ's cognitive function or mood, but at the same time, I want to give him coping tools to make it through the day, to navigate this difficult world.

Pharmacological solutions are a viable option, but this is a deeply personal decision that each family must address for themselves. I never judge another parent for deciding to choose medication. I sure wouldn't want anyone to judge me. We face enough scrutiny as it is. Autism parents often want to try everything and anything, and we are often criticized for that.

When I travel the world speaking and connecting with families, one of the questions I get asked most is on the topic of medication. Our kids have so much to deal with as they get older. Many issues crop up along this journey—depression, aggression, regression, anxiety, OCD. All of these can complicate the picture and create more hurdles. I always encourage parents to do what they think is best for their child's individual circumstances. Every child has different needs. Like every mom, I do the best I can with what I have.

An uncertain future approaches. As RJ nears adulthood, I can't help but ask the universe what will become of my son. Will he go to college, live in a group home, or stay with us as an adult? And what will happen to him when my husband, Rodney, and I are gone? These things also keep me up at night, blinking into the predawn hours.

I am a proactive, tenacious, and resourceful mother for sure, but there are moments when I feel completely paralyzed with worry about my boy's future. Then I have moments of fierce advocacy, as when I took my son to the local police station to introduce him, praying that if they see him bouncing around the neighborhood to his daily haunts, maybe they'll be kind. But even my ferocity is no guarantee.

Our hope is that by sharing our journey, as well as experiences from the many awesomely resilient autism families we have encountered over the years, we will open a sorely needed dialogue about navigating the nuances of autism and adolescence.

The typical teen years can be challenging enough. Throw autism in the mix and you have a cocktail that can be extra tough to swallow. These hormone-infused years can lead to increased aggression, depression, and regression.

And the prevalence is swelling. As I am writing, one in sixty-eight children in the United States is diagnosed as having an autism spectrum disorder, according to the US Centers for Disease Control and Prevention. That means that more than fifty thousand kids with autism turn eighteen each year.

One of the biggest challenges in providing understanding and compassionate care to people with an autism spectrum disorder is that needs change from person to person. Autism is individual. It varies from one extreme, where a person needs custodial care for his or her entire life, to the other extreme, where someone is a highly functional, successful person who may just be viewed as "quirky." Either way, how society regards these young people during this time is crucial to their success as they try to navigate this tricky, fast, and complicated world.

The best news is that awareness is spreading. Just a few years ago, parents had absolutely no resources to help them through the challenging teen years. Now there are tool kits, databases, books, and websites, which I've included at the very end of this book.

There's still a long way to go, though, before our society has become consistently and keenly aware and supportive of the tens of thousands of teenagers making this transition. Families need support and compassion now.

My sincerest wish is that this book will ease the journey on the Autism Express and smooth the ride for all of us.

Holly Robinson Peete

ACKNOWLEDGMENTS

FROM HOLLY

Thank you Andrea Pinkney and Scholastic for recognizing that books are so crucial in nurturing the compassion of a society and warding off stigma. Thank you, Jennifer Abelson, for your editorial hand in bringing this book to fruition, and thanks to Mary Claire Cruz for the design of such an evocative book cover, and art direction of the interior pages, which so brilliantly convey autism's dichotomy.

My family is the engine on the Autism Express. It doesn't move without them. Thank you, RJ and Ryan, for teaching me how to be a mom. Rodney, your evolution as a husband and father has been remarkable. I love you. Robinson and Roman, your mom appreciates your amazing "brotherness." You are kind, patient, and loving, just when we need it most. Mom, you are a rock. Edna and Willie, thank you for loving on my kids.

This book is a gift to the families who are on the

Autism Express. The journey can be arduous but I have encountered the best people I know on it.

FROM RYAN

I would like to thank my twin brother, RJ. We've been together from the beginning, and we will be in it until the end. You have been an inspiration to me and everyone who has the pleasure of knowing you. You've beaten so many odds, and continue to be such a powerful voice for those affected with autism. I love being around you and listening to you speak, because every time you open your mouth, I'm always blown away. I'm so proud of the person you've become and I can't wait to see the successful person you will be in the future.

Thank you to my mom, for staying strong throughout the entire process of making this book. A lot of honesty is poured into these pages, which tends to bring up some sensitive subjects. Nonetheless, the world needs this kind of raw truth when it comes to the teenage years of autism. Mom, I really enjoyed making this book with you. You are one of the most important and incredible persons I know, and I can only wish to be just as amazing as you are someday.

Dad, we have had different opinions when it comes to RJ. But as I'm reflecting on where we are now in our father-daughter relationship, I'm really happy with how far we have come, because I think we can both say that it hasn't always been easy. I think that we're learning to listen to each other better. Thanks for allowing me to be honest when creating this book. Your presence and willingness to evolve as a dad is so admirable.

I would also like to thank my younger brothers, Robinson and Roman, for simply being cool people.

And I want to thank my grandparents, Dolores Robinson and Edna and Willie Peete. Thanks to my Uncles Matt and Skip; thanks to Tia Rebecca, my cousins Reeco, Giselle, and Sulana. Thank you, Wilma McDonald.

My family members always support me. I want to extend my thanks to Tim Lee for being there for my brothers and me for almost a decade. Dr. Pam Wiley, thank you for helping prepare RJ for the world with your incredible program for children, teenagers, and young adults.

Andrea Pinkney and Scholastic, thank you for helping this dream become a reality and for supporting our mission to raise autism awareness with this book.

The small idea I had at the age of ten that sparked our first Scholastic book, *My Brother Charlie*, has now evolved into a powerful coming-of-age story, and I cannot possibly thank you enough. Families need to know that these years are not easy. I'm happy that we're breaking the ice; this needs to be done.

FROM RJ

I have autism. I am not defined by autism. I am Rodney Jackson Peete, a cool kid just trying to handle the world. I have had a long journey on the Autism Express. There are times when I just wanted to jump off this crazy train. Never ride it again . . . But I am blessed to have so many people who love me and help me when things get tough.

Ryan, you are the best twin sister ever. You always have my back. Mom and Dad, thank you for never giving up on me. Robinson and Roman, you are pretty awesome little brothers. Grandmommy, Nana, Grandpa, and Wilma, thank you for everything. I love you ALL.

Scholastic, I am grateful to be able to tell my story. Have my voice heard. There are a lot of books about people like me, but you made my book possible.

To kids with autism: I want you to know how special and valuable you are. Never let anyone tell you different. You have a voice. I dedicate this book to kids who do NOT have the support I do. Hang in there.

ABOUT THE AUTHORS

Actress, author, activist, and philanthropist **HOLLY ROBINSON PEETE** is best known for her many hit television shows, but she is most proud of her community work. Since 2000, when Holly received her son's autism diagnosis, she has worked tirelessly to be a voice for families everywhere who are raising children with this disorder.

Holly is the wife of former NFL quarterback Rodney Peete and the working mother of four children. With her husband, Holly founded the HollyRod Foundation, an organization dedicated to offering help and hope through compassionate care to families living with autism and Parkinson's disease.

Holly's popular children's picture book, *My Brother Charlie*, cowritten with her daughter, Ryan Elizabeth, and illustrated by Shane Evans, was an NAACP Image Award winner that has helped educate many about autism acceptance.

RYAN ELIZABETH PEETE is an avid world traveler.

As a student ambassador with the global student travel organization People to People, Ryan has traveled to India, Peru, and Europe, with more exciting world destinations to come. Ryan is interested in service and advocacy for children with special needs. She coauthored her first book, entitled *My Brother Charlie*, at the age of twelve, to help share awareness about autism among school-age children. Ryan enjoys photography, songwriting, and creative writing.

Ryan's twin brother, **RODNEY JACKSON PEETE**, or RJ, is an intern and mentor at the Los Angeles Speech and Language Therapy Center, where he provides support and help to other children on the autism spectrum. Rodney loves music and fantasy sports, and dedicates his spare time to help spread awareness by traveling with his mom and speaking to kids about his experiences living with autism. RJ's mantra is: "I may have autism, but autism doesn't have me."

The Peetes, who live in Beverly Hills, California, invite readers into their bustling family lives on the highly intimate docuseries *For Peete's Sake*, which airs on OWN, the Oprah Winfrey Network.

RESOURCE GUIDE

WEBSITES

For comprehensive information about autism, some core websites are those of OAR (Organization for Autism Research); ACE (Autism Center for Excellence) at Virginia Commonwealth University; and Autism Speaks.

The CDC (Centers for Disease Control and Prevention) website also contains a wealth of information about autism, as well as an extensive list of links to other autism websites and resources.
www.cdc.gov/ncbddd/autism/index.html

Two other websites, IAN (Interactive Autism Network) and the Autism Consortium, bring members of the autism community together with research scientists to collaborate and enrich our knowledge of autism.

Those sites cover all aspects of autism, including the transition from adolescence to adulthood. Other websites that deal with the journey are:

Autism after 16 is an online magazine with information about transition, postsecondary life, employment, housing, finance, health, and more. www.autismafter16.com/content/about-us

Autism Help's website has a section on the teen years that includes information about puberty, sexuality, hygiene, and other sensitive adolescent issues. www.autismhelp.info

Autism Transition Handbook is a website whose mission is to "provide the most current and comprehensive information on the transition to adulthood." The site has a long list of topics and is very welcoming and user-friendly. www.autismhandbook.org/index.php/Main_Page

About.com hosts articles about teens and ASD (Autism Spectrum Disorder), with topics on sexuality, puberty, fostering independence, becoming adults, and handling college and careers.

autism.about.com/od/transitioncollegejobs

Going-to-College has information about living college life with a disability. Designed for high school students, it provides video clips, activities, and additional resources to help students get a head start in planning for college.

http://www.going-to-college.org/overview/index.html

GUIDES AND FACT SHEETS

There is a treasure trove of guides and information booklets for families of teens with ASD who are embarking on the transition to adulthood. Below are some of them.

"A Guide for Transition to Adulthood" is a booklet in the series Life Journey through Autism, created by Danya International and OAR. The guide can be downloaded or a print copy ordered from the OAR website.

www.researchautism.org/resources/reading/index.asp

"Adolescents and ASD," a page on the ACE website, offers a comprehensive list of resources to help families, professionals, and persons with ASD navigate the transition.
www.vcuautismcenter.org/resources/adolescence.cfm

"Autism Spectrum Disorder and the Transition to Adulthood" is available on the Virginia Department of Education website. The booklet has comprehensive information about transition assessment and planning, adult services, postsecondary education, employment, home living skills, and Social Security and benefits planning.
www.doe.virginia.gov/special_ed/disabilities/autism /technical_asst_documents/autism_transition.pdf

Community-based Skills Assessment (CSA) is a tool for parents and professionals to assess the skill levels and abilities of persons with ASD, beginning at age twelve and continuing into adulthood, to enable them to develop a comprehensive plan. The CSA was created by Autism Speaks in collaboration with Virginia

Commonwealth University's Rehabilitation Research and Training Center. The first URL below provides information about using the CSA, and the second URL is the pdf for downloading.

www.autismspeaks.org/family-services/community -based-skills-assessment?utm_source=email

http://www.vcuautismcenter.org/documents/Final CommunityAssessment711141.pdf

Employment guides are free on the website of Forward Motion Coaching, which specializes in career counseling for persons with Asperger's syndrome, non-verbal learning disorders, and other communication challenges.

www.forwardmotion.info/wp/free-guides

Postsecondary Educational Opportunities Guide is a tool kit from Autism Speaks that helps to explore the opportunities and learning environments after leaving school.

www.autismspeaks.org/family-services/tool-kits /postsecondary

"Preparing to Experience College Living," a fact sheet from the Autism Society, has tips on learning to live independently and developing academic and social skills.

https://www.autismspeaks.org/docs/family_services_docs/CollegeLiving.pdf

"Puberty and Autism Spectrum Disorder," an information sheet from Autism Victoria on their Amaze website, gives detailed advice to parents on how to help their children through this confusing time. It also lists other resources on puberty.

www.amaze.org.au/uploads/2011/08/Fact-Sheet-Puberty-and-Autism-Spectrum-Disorders-Aug-2011.pdf

Transition to Adulthood Guidelines is a series by OCALI (Ohio Center for Autism and Low Incidence) on transitioning to adulthood, including age-appropriate assessment, employment, IEP transition information, and school-age programming.

www.ocali.org/project/transition_to_adulthood_guidelines

Transition Tool Kit by Autism Speaks covers self-advocacy, transition plans, community living, employment options, housing, legal matters, and more.
https://www.autismspeaks.org/family-services/tool-kits/transition-tool-kit

EDUCATION AND TRAINING

Following is only a very small sample of the opportunities available for education and training.

For those of you who would like to delve into the autism research that's being done—happily, there is a great deal of it—an invaluable aid is "A Parent's Guide to Research." This is a detailed how-to (and where), complete with worksheets for your use. It was written by Danya International, OAR, and SARRC (Southwest Autism Research and Resource Center), and is available on the OAR website.
http://www.researchautism.org/resources/parents%20guide.pdf

ACE's website offers a variety of videos, online courses and seminars, and other training and education formats to meet the needs of both family members and professionals.

http://www.vcuautismcenter.org/te/index.cfm

The BILT Course: Building Independent Lives through Training (formerly AGI Residential/Daily Living Support Course) provides parents, siblings, family members, in-home support workers, agency support providers, and volunteers from the community with the knowledge, skills, and tools to support the daily living needs of transition-age students and older. The course is online and is not free.

http://www.houltoninstitute.com/programs/agi -residential-daily-living-support-course/

VIDEOS AND ADDITIONAL SUPPORT INFORMATION

Living with Asperger's: A Video about Life on the Spectrum is the first part of a three-part video series covering experiences of people with ASD. The focus is on Asperger's syndrome although it is not limited to that. It's available on YouTube.

www.youtube.com/watch?v=MJUGcvYE-nc

The Social Group II is a 2012 honors thesis/documentary project by Duke University students, about a group of teenagers with high-functioning autism who have been meeting every Friday for the past ten years. It's available on YouTube.
www.youtube.com/watch?v=1jbP5JK3Nes

"Young Adults with Autism Can Thrive in High-Tech Jobs," a story on careers for people with ASD, is available on the website of NPR, where it aired April 22, 2013.
www.npr.org/sections/health-shots/2013/04/22
/177452578/young-adults-with-autism-can-thrive-in
-high-tech-jobs

Some adolescents with ASD may need significant help handling the intensity of their emotions during adolescence and may also face depression and thoughts of suicide. The National Suicide Prevention Lifeline provides free and confidential support twenty-four hours a day, seven days a week. For immediate help, call 1-800-273-8255 (TALK), to be connected with a skilled, trained counselor at a crisis center in your area.
www.suicidepreventionlifeline.org